April 22 1993

A Doctor's Journey

*Happy Birthday
on your
the story journey*

A Doctor's Journey

The Chronos Directive

Robert Klein, M.D.,
and
William Bryant

VANTAGE PRESS
New York

FIRST EDITION

All rights reserved, including the right of reproduction in whole or in part in any form.

Copyright © 1993 by Robert Klein, M.D.

Published by Vantage Press, Inc.
516 West 34th Street, New York, New York 10001

Manufactured in the United States of America
ISBN: 0-533-10192-1

Library of Congress Catalog Card No.: 91-91563

0 9 8 7 6 5 4 3 2 1

Contents

I.	The Chronos Directive	1
II.	Basal Themes	11
III.	The New World	49
IV.	Constriction and Release	86
V.	The Arc of Redemption	111

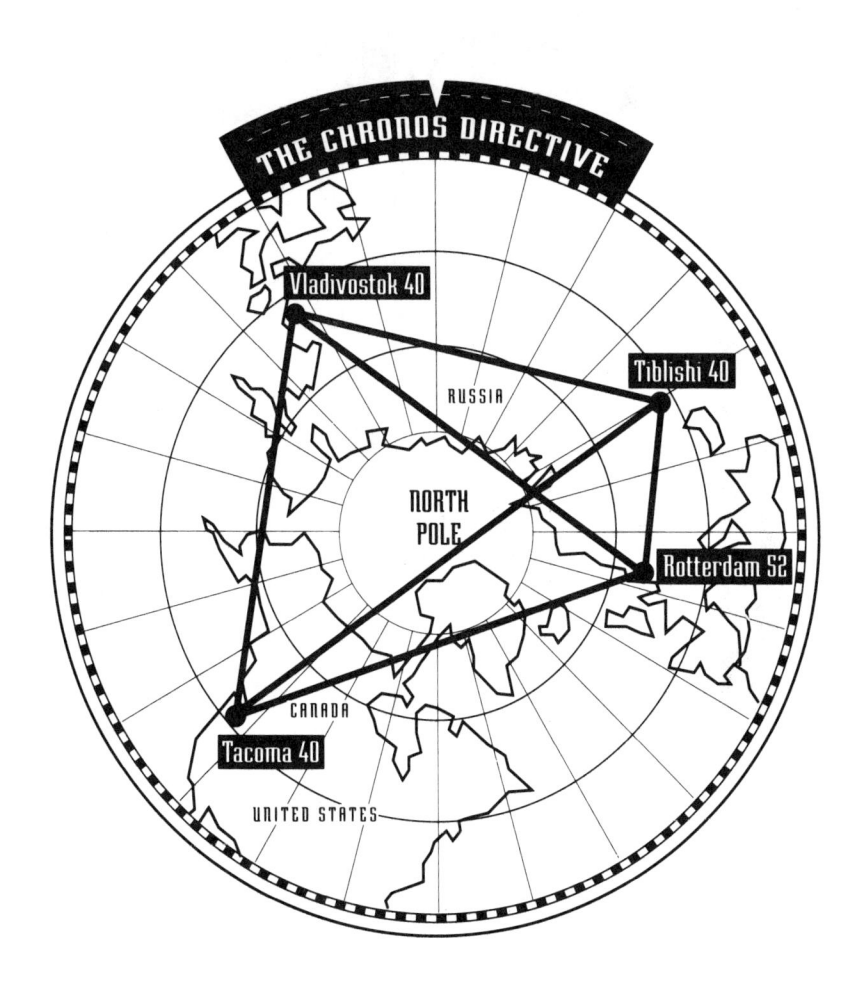

THE CHRONOS DIRECTIVE

- Vladivostok 40
- Tiblishi 40
- Rotterdam 52
- Tacoma 40

RUSSIA
NORTH POLE
CANADA
UNITED STATES

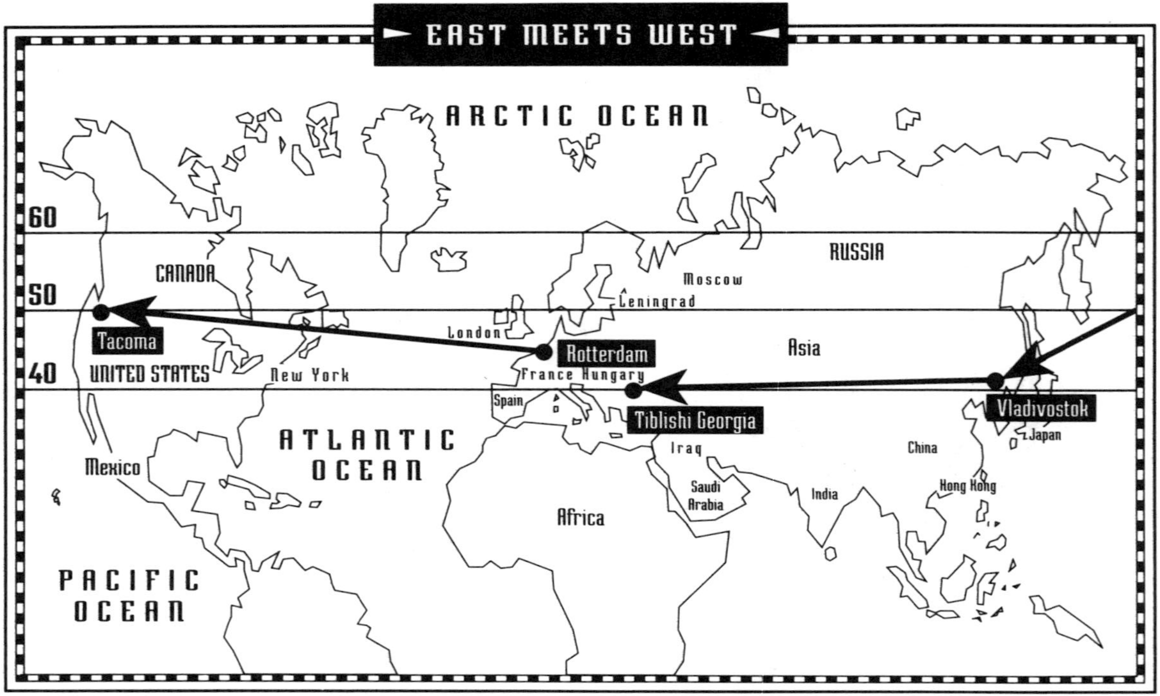
EAST MEETS WEST
ARCTIC OCEAN
60
50
40
RUSSIA
CANADA
Moscow
Leningrad
London
Tacoma
Rotterdam
Asia
UNITED STATES
New York
France
Hungary
Spain
Tiblishi Georgia
Vladivostok
Japan
ATLANTIC OCEAN
Mexico
Iraq
China
Saudi Arabia
India
Hong Kong
Africa
PACIFIC OCEAN

LIFE SPAN
30 YEAR CYCLE

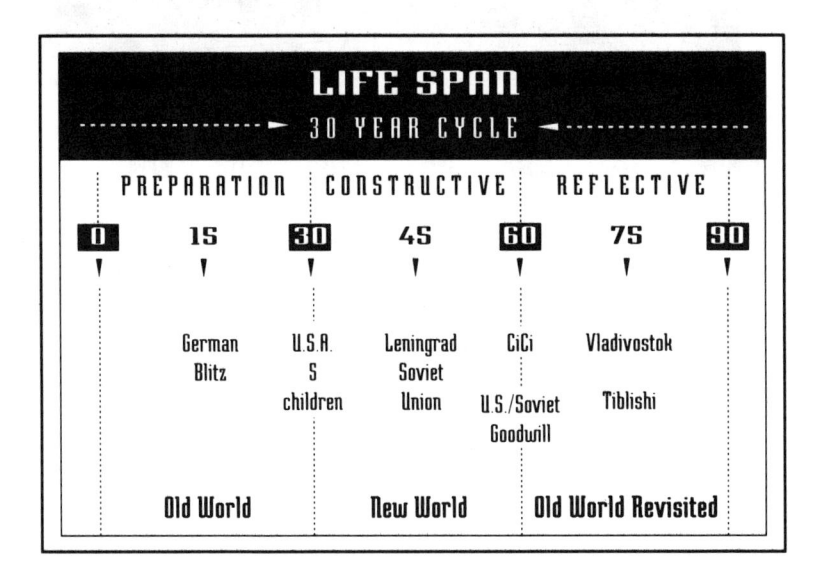

PREPARATION	CONSTRUCTIVE	REFLECTIVE

0 — 15 — **30** — 45 — **60** — 75 — **90**

	German Blitz	U.S.A. 5 children	Leningrad Soviet Union	CiCi U.S./Soviet Goodwill	Vladivostok Tiblishi	

Old World | **New World** | **Old World Revisited**

CAREER
12 YEAR CYCLE

0	12	**24**	36	**48**	60	**72**	84
Gymnasium Haariem	Leyoen Medicine	Allenmore Medical Center	Recertification Seattle	Personal Injuries Legal		Russia Medical Building	
Montessori Haariem	Deift Naval Architecture	TGH Intern Tacoma	Board Certification New York	Recertification Portland	Seattle Design Comp.		
Gymnasium Haariem		House	Puget Tower Apartments		Sheffield Apt.	Medal of Honor and Freedom to the City of Vladvosk	
Evert T-Ford			Crystal Mt. Ski Cabin	Allenmore Center Management	N. Light House Condo		
				Allenmore Ridge Condo Lake Chelan Hi Tide Ocean			

INDIVIDUAL PSYCHOLOGICAL CRISES
► 7 YEAR CYCLE—[0-42] ◄

0	7	14	21	28	35	42
	Montessori	Gymnasium Exam WWII	Delft War Neurosis Interrogations	M.D. Leyden Exam	Holland Revisited	Board Exam
Sport Competition		Home Beach/ Dunes	Marriage Rowing Crew Laga Stroke		Ski Crystal Mountain	Vietnam War
			Sailboat			Cal 34 Sailboat Dutch Flute

► 7 YEAR CYCLE—[49-92] ◄

49	56	63	70	77	84	92
Recert. Exam	Recert. Exam	Burn out Depression Stress Syndrome	Heart Condition	Meditation		
	Welfare Fraud					
Bart Finance	Divorce	Ethics Biofeedback				
Sail Ski Racing	Tennis	Goodwill Physicians Exchange				
		Ski Sun Valley Design				
	Soccer Stars	Competition				

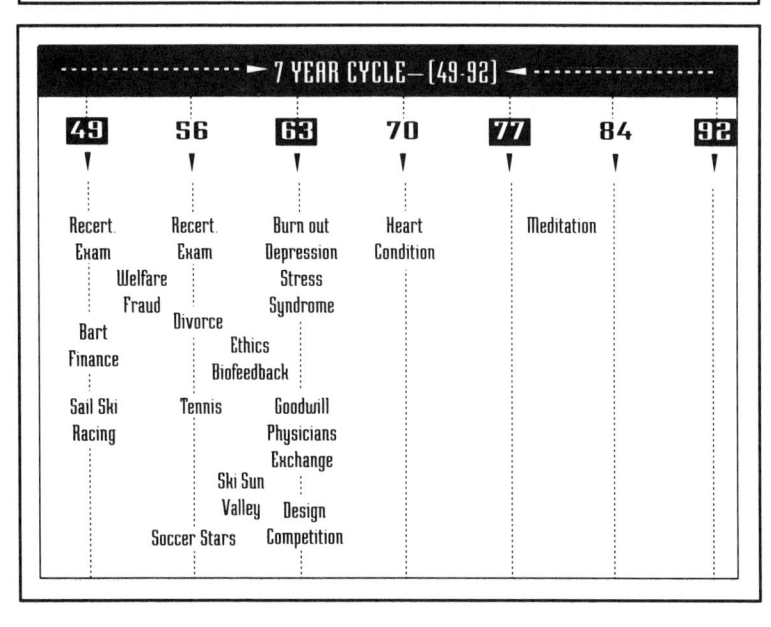

A Doctor's Journey

Chapter I
The Chronos Directive

I am Chronos, the Spirit of Time, the Spirit of the Age, the Lord of the Measures. I am the Indicator, the Lord of Necessity, the regent of your passing time. My hand binds the threads between sowing and reaping, seeding and fruiting, cause and effect, birth and death, on the loom of evolution.

Whosoever enters my stream shall follow its course from the before to the after. Be not afeared—I am your servant. As the weaver of your tapestry of coming and going, I shall connect your past to your future, your trek towards freedom. As the sage said for me, "He who will, I lead. He who won't, I drag." I govern the phase, the period, the epoch, the aeon. I orchestrate your search for experience and its assimilation. Thus, I bring the gift of your crisis. How else shall you discover yourselves?

Do not fear me, though ofttimes I wear the mantle of chaos and the countenance of severity. I am the time that cracks the rigid bulwark of your institutions. I am the spiral of evolution hidden within all revolution for I govern both the ascent and the collapse of civilizations. You have recognized me in your great myths as the grave Father of your time.

Do not run from me. Heed me! Your vanishing creams, your hormone injections, your time and motion graphs, your lethargy, your impatience, your insurance policies, your "get-rich-quick" frolics, your fear of aging cannot escape me. You dare not kill me without maiming your eternity. Financiers speculate with me, fashions condemn me, physicians seek to confound me, politicians pray to me, youth try to kill me, physicists seek to reverse me, athletes try to outrun me—but who understands me?

I pray you, do not thrash about on your hook of time; better you should understand me and heed my message; better you should uncover my wisdom and learn to live well in time.

I must inform you, some measure of your time runneth out. The cycle of apocalyptic time has reached you, and the bells of warning toll the departing age. Oh, hear me! Put not your faith in systems. Follow not the mindless mob nor glittering utopias. Beware the chameleon of the public mind! Grieve not for the past. Spill not the blood in the name of change, but learn from me in you. It is thy past that shapes thy future. It is thy future that shapes thy present. Time offers treasures in the cloak of misfortune. Blame not your spouse, your boss, your parents and genetic ancestors, the fall of the dollar, the gyrations of government for your predicaments and obstacles; make not false enemies.

I, Chronos, seek nothing more than to arouse in you a richer perception of your time. It is within your soul that time regenerates its warnings and its potential. This is the crucible where past meets future in the alchemical fire of your self-transmutation. This is your source of revivifying hope and empowered courage. This is the well where you shall draw the elixir of love and pour it into the chalice of the world. So, too, shall you forge a fresh sword on the anvil of your time to clear the illusions festooning your present. Decode time and you shall fathom destiny;

fathom destiny and you shall know freedom. I tell you, your time-life is your masterwork. I shall instruct you. I shall tell you a story. Remember well, I give you your greatest gift—your story. Without a story of your own, you cannot exist. Thus, I shall serve you: you who are the wounded in spirit, you who are trapped in the dungeon of your NOW, you who lie becalmed on the horizonless sea, you who have mislaid your sense of path, you who lie paralyzed in illusions of worthlessness, you who spin in a vortex of disruption, I offer you a draft of hope. Know me! I am the order, not the creator. It is your indivisible self who is the true helmsman, though you know it not. Only you can be the master of your future. And so it is.

* * *

This February night in 1989 was starlit, crisp, and cold. An arctic wind cut through the avenues of mute automobiles in the deserted car park of the Tacoma Dome. Jan was anxious. The snowstorm that day had threatened the arrival of a young soccer team from Moscow, and the dangerous roads meant that the attendance would suffer. Being a financial supporter of the local indoor soccer team, he was concerned about its survival. As he picked his way gingerly across the gleaming ice to the entrance, a shard of remembrance, nudged free by the scrunch of his feet, touched his awareness, a fleeting image of another snowy night on the eastern front in Hungary, in March of 1945. This disconcerting image vanished when he opened the door and the dazzling intensity of the dome bombarded his senses. He made his way through the noise and flickering laser lights to his favorite spot behind the goal, close to the action, where he could watch his team play the inexperienced Soviets. Jan always enjoyed the excitement. Indoor soccer has its own belligerent mood—high-speed action, lasers, numbing decibel levels, rapid plays from end to end. But this time something was different—he felt different.

This night the atmosphere stirred something within him triggered by the grunts, as bodies slammed against the boards, the entanglement of arms and legs, the smell of sweat, the urgency, the shouts in the Russian tongue. Again, gruesome images erupted in the cauldron of his mental imagery. Old phantoms broke free from the chains of time past to race among his emotions. These were ancient visions, yet alive with disturbing energy—of dirt and snow, blood and stench. As Jan's past hurtled into his present, so he felt the taste of fear on his tongue, the quake of heavy artillery, shouts of screaming Russian infantry overrunning the German defenses in Hungary in that snowy spring of 1945. Without warning, his now and his then were one. He felt the need to escape.

Then he was a young Dutchman of seventeen trapped on special assignment on the eastern front with the German SS. Now he was a 63-year-old doctor trapped in a sinister time warp—living in two worlds at once. Why were these phantoms so real? These flashbacks had a life of their own, as if Jan's psyche were at war with his rational mind.

After the game, he went to a reception for the players, officials, and promoters. Usually, he felt at ease with the energy and warmth of such gatherings, stimulated by the communality of deserved success. This time, however, he felt decidedly uneasy. The aftermath of the flashbacks had unsettled him, dampened his natural spirits and usual sociability. He moved in a hesitant orbit among the guests, drink in hand—an ungainly mesh of mumbling, listening, munching. Communication was a problem with these high-spirited, fresh-faced, ravenous Russians.

Suddenly, another disconnected fragment of memory broke free. The song "Lili Marlene" rose from some subterranean chamber to haunt him, a song sung by both friend and foe alike in the trenches, the drinking places, the marching columns of the Great War. He was now acutely aware of his disorientation. He looked into the faces as he moved among them. *Do I know you? Have we met? Were you friend? Were you foe?* he wondered. A turbulent mix of apprehension and disjointed thought distracted him, as outer and inner worlds swirled together in his uncertain present. Everything was a surrealistic shamble of bits and pieces. He noticed the unusually large bifocals of the Soviet representative of the Goodwill Games. Always susceptible to the feminine presence, he was drawn to the charming interpreter working so intently in the staccatic pauses to keep the flow going. He also met the administrator of his hospital, with whom he had worked twenty-four years earlier on the design of his hospital. They talked for a while about plans to celebrate the twenty-fifth anniversary, but Jan's rational thinking refused to focus.

The reception, the warmth, and the companionship did nothing to settle or soothe him. He was just not himself. What was this thing gnawing away at his equanimity? Here he stood with so many of the autumnal blessings of life. Jan had partially retired from his medical practice. His family had grown up. A new romance had blossomed in his sixtieth year and brought him a child to restore his enthusiasm for life. Financially secure after decades of hard work, sacrifice, and astute speculation, he could now afford to support his favorite projects. He owned several condominiums in the city and resort homes in the mountains and on the coast. Tennis and sailing kept his health in a robust condition, and his various club memberships brought Jan much social pleasure. Yet despite all the blessings of maturity, his universe was coming apart at the seams. Some rogue enzyme was eating away at the very fabric of his peace of mind. There were disturbing problems in his medical practice, and his family life was rapidly turning sour. Jan felt pressured and uneasy, and his desperate sessions with a psychiatrist only made him feel even more on edge and fearful. What the devil was happening?

Jan's turbulence continued when his partner and friends urged him to see a much-vaunted movie. He went and again stumbled into another furor of emotion. The film was centered on the Russian invasion of Budapest in 1956. He cringed in his seat, recoiling from the images of street fighting, the grimness and horror, the monstrous, squirming tanks clanking and grinding their way through the women and children, the blood and smoke. Old recognitions assaulted him. There, on the screen, was the miserably debased officer flagrantly manipulating and abusing women. He saw the tortured souls buffeted by war, acting and reacting with no care for tomorrow. He knew them—he had been one of them. Overcome by repulsion, he could do nothing but escape by rushing from the theater for a breath of fresh air and a walk in solitude.

Yet another event at this time battered Jan's rapidly eroding confidence. His mate had booked a flight to the East for herself and their infant on a DC-10. A week before their departure, his TV screen showed the horrendous moment of impact as a DC-10 went down in Chicago. These vivid images threw open the doors to another anteroom in his soul. The burnt and mutilated children brought back terrifying nights of fear, nights when Allied bombers carpet-bombed wide swathes across German cities, saturating them in flames. Jan was aware of their approach, the throbbing engines, the high-pitched screams of falling bombs, the crashing planes—bombs and planes aimed directly at him. How could he let his child fly, knowing there was so little protection? "In cases of emergency, hold your child in your lap or put it on the floor." His panic created dissention with his mate, and again he felt compelled to rush from his apartment. He always had to escape—escape meant survival.

Then came the San Francisco earthquake, its vivid television images compelling Jan to relive the collapsing bridges across the Rhine, blasted by Allied bombers or destroyed by the retreating troops. He, too, had been on the run, crossing the perilous river as a furtive youth deserting his unit, fleeing from the SS only to fall into the clutches of the Americans.

The stress of all this, accentuated by difficulties in Jan's medical practice and the rising antagonism in his family life, forced him to visit a psychiatrist. But again, his confounded past would not release him. Here he was again, eye to eye with an interrogator. Damn all those interrogators—his father, the American military, the FBI, the Dutch officials—clever, manipulating minds, probing, tripping, and trapping him. It was all too much.

Despite being daily tossed about by the rabid hounds of emotion, fresh and unexpected opportunities presented themselves. Jan's meetings with the Soviets at the soccer reception, combined with the approaching Goodwill Games, offered him a new direction. He was excited by the prospect of developing a scheme to foster the exchange of Soviet and American doctors. The first meetings would be coordinated with the Goodwill Games in the Pacific Northwest.

Jan set to work with his customary singlemindedness and tenacity. He had a new project; he always had to have a project to channel his interior drive. The physician exchange was absolutely new—nothing existed except an idea, one perfectly attuned to the times. Jan soon managed to assemble a motley assortment of individuals and groups made up of doctors, bankers, and pharmaceutical representatives. Many problems had to be solved. How could the transport be organized? Who would pay for it all? Could they communicate with the Soviets despite the erratic telephone system? Would the shaky hand of glasnost suddenly slam the doors?

The path to realization was strewn with the broken glass of controversy; but, slowly, the ideas solidified and a program was devised to cover sports medicine, nuclear controls, the medical effects of Chernobyl and Hanford, global medicine, and cardiac research.

Jan became utterly frustrated at times. He sat in meetings for hours, his back aching, eyes watering, while grandiose and verbose fantasies were hatched with little regard for reality, especially the dwindling time. He found it difficult to keep his temper in check. Some individuals obviously hoped to enhance their own political ambition; others were seeking social prestige. Sessions of argument and counterargument threatened to disperse the venture. Nothing would hold together, and Jan would return home exhausted and dispirited.

* * *

I, Chronos, have set the stage of Jan's destiny as his sixty-third year forms itself into a crisis of major proportions. The fearsome vultures of his past have returned to roost in the branches of his present, and the cohesion of his life breaks down. His crisis demands attention, insists on being recognized, examined, corrected, and cleared. Yet it is also a threshold of opportunity, if only he meets the psychological conditions. All this is nothing less than the causal metabolism of the psyche disrupting Jan's status quo in the name of growth.

Mark well, the creative currents of the future also swirl in his maelstrom. Though cloaked in illusion's chaos and accident, Jan's future generates itself in his present. The reception is the fertile soil wherein is seeded ideas that will germinate and formulate themselves into events touching many lives. This moment is the inscrutable crucible of synchrony wherein was manifest the idea to promote the exchange of American and eastern-bloc physicians. Thus, the moment is a point of genesis in the midst of apparent chaos.

Be assured, then, that all is in order. Regardless of turbulence and disorientation, Jan is in perfect accord with the rhythms of his time, as destiny, known only to his unconscious self, remorselessly drives him onward.

Consider well the fact that Jan is not a closed entity, a self-contained system. His life is synchronized with the lives of others and even changes in the planetary mind—what Huxley called "the mind at large." Emerson, too, was correct when he recognized the mysterious tie between person and event. See now how Jan's destiny confronts him with a crucial question: Can he fashion friendship with old adversaries who once, in a mere blink of historical time, had tried to destroy him? The essential answer pivots on Jan's ability to transmute his past.

At this point I shall introduce one of my tools of destiny—an instrument engraved with my name—"synchronicity." With this Jan positioned himself in the right place at the propitious moment.

The stage is the 1990 Goodwill Games held in the Pacific Northwest. Such events are always more than they seem. It is here that I, the spirit of the coming age, exert my influence. It is here that the cross-pollination of ideas and ideals can dissolve the hoary citadels of nationalism, eroding the boundaries that separate one from another. Here, in the cradle of human interaction, self can meet self, mind to mind, heart to heart. This exchange exemplifies the true synergy between East and West. It is on this greater stage of the mesocosm that our sibling of time has stumbled—the sleepwalker who would wake himself. And so it is.

Chapter II
Basal Themes

Jan's parents met in their undergraduate years at Holland's most historic and prestigious university, one of the oldest in Europe. Leiden gloried in its aura of past scholastic and scientific luminaries. Surrounded by vibrant fields of tulips, the town is sectioned by its café-lined canals. The Rhine, the continental river of life, flows through it. Holland's oldest refuge, the small hill called the Burcht (fort) was its birthplace long ago in ancient Saxon times. Rembrandt and many pioneers of science have walked its cobbled streets. Linnaeus, the great botanist, worked in the botanical gardens, and Hugyens, Fahrenheit, and Leeuwenhoek added to its illustrious memory.

Cornelia was a slender, intelligent, soft-spoken, and attractive woman of twenty-two; her countenance was comfortably proportioned, with a finely shaped nose and gentle, perceptive, dark brown eyes suffused with a hint of melancholia. Willem, in strong contrast, was angular, with an intellectual, high-framed brow, and the penetrating eyes of an analyst. Quick and alert in movement and supple-minded, he could be patriarchal, cold, caustic, concentrated, yet emotional, witty, and charming.

Jan, the first-born of five children, entered mortal space and time in the Rotterdam of 1927. This old seaport, with its long-standing maritime lineage, was one of the world's foremost commercial hubs. Its harbor was always crammed with neatly packed rows of barges and parallel queues of oceanic freighters waiting patiently to load or unload. Imperious tugs hauled the barges off the Rhine past great grain elevators, coal mountains, offices, warehouses, and derricks. It was a panoramic view softened by the smokestacks of the ascendant age of the steamship. You could taste the incense of industry—the smoke, coal, and grain dust, the oil and diesel fumes.

Much of Rotterdam's vitality surged along its restless waterfront, teeming with sailors from Japan, China, India, and Vietnam, not to mention those from western ports. The mood of the waterfront seeped into Jan's embryonic bliss, soon to be reinforced while being pushed about in his stroller through the incoherent bedlam of many strange tongues.

Jan's parents lived in the red-light district of Katendrecht, where Willem had a cramped office in their small house. Here he ministered to an endless supply of medical emergencies, except when rushing from ship to ship—which was often, since the danger of infectious diseases like smallpox was ever present. Willem was often frustrated by his lack of equipment, forcing him to send his patients to the hospital laboratory whenever X rays and tests were necessary. His experiences with the deprived, the prostitutes, the opium addicts, and the unemployed generated his deepening concern for the poor and downtrodden. These formative experiences awakened his interest in socialized medicine, not to mention a fierce antagonism against the authoritarian and exploitive capitalists of the age.

Jan was born prematurely without the presence of his father, who had been quarantined for six weeks by the measles. The baby's first year was disrupted by numerous episodes of colic. Later, his slowness in learning to speak made his parents suspect some kind of retardation. It was Jan's sister, Machteld, born a year later, who did all the talking.

Jan was three when his family moved to a country village. Here the little lad spent most of his time with the farmers and their animals. His retarded speech remained a source of concern, but he did display an early mechanical bent. Willem owned a Model-T Ford complete with a mechanic. When given some tools, the happy lad would disappear under the chassis and proceed to make all the necessary imitative adjustments.

Jan was never allowed to settle in one place for very long—a recurrent theme in his first thirty years. Time and time again he was torn away from any kind of environmental security and unripened friendship with his peers. Willem, through his daily exposure to all kinds of aberrant behavior in his medical work, perhaps enhanced by his own sexual fixations, became increasingly drawn to the utopian phantasm of Freudian psychology. As part of his training, he began his residency program in psychiatric medicine in a fortresslike compound, complete with tiny, barred windows, towering walls, and a moat bristling with wicked stakes and barbed wire. Outside all this was yet another perimeter of defense—earthworks and guards.

Doctors, their families, and the criminal psychopaths were all sequestered together, there being little separation between the normal and abnormal—the doctors were the ones wearing white coats. Jan could always recall the outlandish mood of that place, the vivid strangeness of the inmates—the obliqueness of their logic, their odd compulsions. He remembered the screams of his mother when she discovered one hiding under her bed. The bewildered five year old would also never forget the sharp verbal exchanges of the white coats and the bitter quarreling of his parents. Life in the asylum was a procession of emergencies, marked by jarring alarm bells when someone escaped and had to be hunted down by the police. Occasionally, he managed to slip away, to run along the dike walls—breathing liberty and normality. The atmosphere of the asylum would haunt him all his days and be recurrently reinforced later on.

Jan attended the village school, where the son of a doctor, especially one from the asylum, was regarded as an alien. The school dress code insisted that everyone wear black socks. Jan, however, hated these things with a passion and at first refused to conform. This was his first attempt at rebellion, and it brought him nothing but ridicule and mockery.

Willem was a brilliant yet complicated man. Devoted to his patients, he also adored opera and was a marvelous teller of tales. His rapierlike wit, however, always had a corkscrew on the end—just enough of a twist to hurt and keep his friends at a cool distance. As his political leanings turned more toward socialism, so he became increasingly at odds with his colleagues. In those days, neurology and psychiatry were uneasy partners.

Willem's interests, however, graduated from the dissection of the body, to the dissection of the psyche. The family dining room served as his laboratory or, as Jan saw it, his interrogation room. Jan always felt apprehensive in his father's presence, rapidly wilting under his withering psychological interrogation whenever anything went wrong; indeed, Willem's connection to his son was largely analytical and heavily authoritarian. Willem was as much a stranger to Jan as he was to his own remote, statuesque, heart-hidden father.

Fascinated by human behavior, particularly its criminal aspects, Willem took delight in applying Freudian techniques to his young son. The result of this abstract and aggressive intellectualizing merely filled the bewildered boy with a massive load of indigestible guilt—enough to torpedo a lifetime of relationships. When Jan fell off his bicycle and badly grazed his knees, Willem met the tearful lad, saying, "So you fell off? Make sure you learn from this, Jan. You did this to yourself; only you are responsible. This is how you teach yourself. Something in you made you do it."

This was typical of Willem's aloof manner. He always gave cerebral retorts, never the comfort of the heart's warmth. The result of this, reinforced time and time again, built his son's self-doubt. When told of Jan's poor examination performance, Willem confronted him, stressing the point that Jan had brought this upon himself deliberately, to wake himself. He always presented the idea that the boy was at odds with himself, even in conflict with his own unconscious self and its drives. No matter how hard Jan tried, he could never find a way to win his father's approval.

Cornelia was kind and sympathetic, but she was mostly preoccupied with her own extreme mood swings. Much of her natural gentleness of soul was occluded by crying spells and the depression wrought by her precarious marriage. She felt very much a victim of Willem's demands, and her frequent breakdowns put her in the sanitorium from time to time. Jan tried to support her after each domestic quarrel, but his innocence inevitably got caught in the injurious crossfire. Jan could never understand why both his parents turned on him, although, decades later Jan was convinced his father was jealous of him.

The family eventually left the asylum and went to Vienna, the birthplace of the Freudian mind. Here his father could immerse himself in study with those intense and prickly disciples of the master. They traveled by train with their enormous St. Bernard, who trampled all over the five-year-old boy; their curious antics on the carriage floor made the passengers assume they were circus folk. The Vienna episode, however, was short-lived and off they sped again. There were countless places, strange sights, so many peculiar languages—Jan could not understand a word—travelling everywhere, he belonged nowhere.

Willem completed his training at Leiden, then established a practice in Haarlem. Jan and Machteld were sent to a public school, again finding themselves incarcerated in a gloomy building with tiny windows. As usual, his repressive school life interfered with his education, but Jan did get claustrophobia and plenty of headaches. It seemed to him as if gloom was always synonymous with authority, rigidity, and control. Cornelia, however, recognized the cause of Jan's suffering and promptly sent him to a Montessori school. Here he flourished in liberty—there were hardly any rules at all. Mathematics, in particular, fascinated Jan, and this was the only study he pursued. Later, when he reached high school, Jan found himself lagging years behind in his language skills. Willem was now very strict about his son's studies, and the boy spent many a summer afternoon in his room while his family enjoyed the beach. At least he had his own room—and the pigeons he shared with Machteld.

Early in 1939, Europe began to flinch as the Reich, now empowered by the industrial metabolism of the Ruhr, flexed its diplomatic muscles. Fear hovered around every dinner table in Europe. Jan's father, however, was sympathetic to Germany's drive to free itself from the fetters of Western capitalism and the growing threat of a smothering communism. Willem was not then a member of the Nationalist Socialist Party, supported by about 3 percent of the Dutch electorate; but as an energetic socialist, he urged reform, acutely aware as he was of the terrible social neglect following the First World War.

Jan did not join in the dinner discussions dominated by his father, who tended to pontificate. Jan was not a talker, anyway. He had his own immediate problems and interests. His attendance at the local gymnasium resurrected his old claustrophobia. It was always the same—how to fit in, how to obey the system, how to submit to authority. But he did have his grand compensation, his own wings of freedom—a horse.

Galloping alone among the dunes, along the beach and shallows, Jan's soul and senses merged with the salted breeze and open horizon. Jan had adopted a horse, an Arabian, his instructor being an aggressive, sergeant-major-like fellow, whose uncompromising severity had frightened Machteld away. But Jan learned well for he had great need of this equestrian escape to freedom. Learning the sensitivity of the reins and knees, Jan was delighted to feel the exhilaration of life beneath and within him. How he relished his brief moments of liberty—but they would not last.

* * *

I am Chronos, and I have scored for you the formative agents in Jan's beginning. These are the basal themes reverberating throughout his lifespan. Be assured such experiences never sink into the depths of oblivion. View them as energy vortexes, causal impulses, seeds that will germinate in future seasons.

Know well, a childhood bereft of my time order is simply inconceivable. Does not childhood demonstrate to you an exquisite wisdom of unfolding stages whereby the indivisible self incorporates, precipitates itself in time and space? This way you construct the foundation for independence and destiny. Yes, this emergence of selfhood is dependent on my rhythmicity. So, please consider the fact that you yourself display a multitude of my cycles. You are a complex confederacy of biological clocks, responsible for your well-being, your sleep patterns, glandular secretions, immune cycles, temperature fluctuations, tissue repair, indeed, all cycles in your respiration and metabolism. Just try a heavy meal at three o'clock in the morning—you will get my point. Furthermore, any serious discord in the symphony of organic rhythms will eventually sow the seeds of disease. Sadly, the therapies restoring displaced time systems have yet to appear. But they will!

You acknowledge my presence in your organic nature but are blind to the fact that I am also the fundamental agent in your psychological life and the very chronography of your destiny. It is easy to see why this is ignored. The problem is that you are impaled on the narrow spike you call NOW with all its demands, dilemmas, pleasures, and pains. It is easy to lose your sense of span, your feeling of continuity. No wonder you may think your life is a haphazard affair—just one damn thing after another. No wonder you may feel shaped by accident, a marionette of circumstance, or the plaything of your genes. No wonder you lose sight of the magnificent breadth of your existence and the purposeful stream of destiny flowing within it. No wonder you are prey to illusions, which sap your confidence and energy. So remember well my presence in you. Remember, too, that the nutriment of your experience must be digested. I, Chronos, work in the cause and effect of your pilgrimage from the before to the after.

Mark well the fact that you are not a closed system, the separate, isolated entity you assume yourself to be. Of course, you are so in your space, but not so in your time, wherein your life is inextricably meshed with the cycles of other human beings, your nation, the planet itself. As I shall demonstrate for you, Jan's time was about to intersect the apocalyptic cycles of Europe, thus constructing a version of hell, a vast complex of experience to be assimilated later. And so it is.

* * *

The German invasion and the collapse of Holland were almost instantaneous. The Dutch half-heartedly believed their own "Maginot Line," their intricate network of dikes, when flooded, would block the highly mechanized invaders. But Hitler's blitzkreig, the panzer punch, a concept first suggested by a young French officer by the name of Charles de Gaulle, swallowed Holland whole in five days.

Jan's first brush with war was peripheral but near enough. The fifteen year old watched a serene morning sky fill with the white puffs of parachutes, then heard the sirens, a few shots, and distant detonations. He was in little danger since Haarlem was not strategically situated and the intruders concentrated on controlling the railway stations, road intersections, and bridges. The royal family fled to England, and many ships escaped from Rotterdam despite the bombing blockade.

The suddenness of the attack set everyone's emotionality at a higher notch. Jan felt more excitement than fear as the mysterious and illogical adult world intruded upon the natural self-preoccupations of adolescence. Daily life soon returned to a semblance of order as the people settled uneasily under the German thumb. Ration books were issued and the schools reopened. Jan could no longer cycle on the roads crammed with westward moving horse-drawn gun carriages, motorcycles, troop trucks, and the occasional tank.

Jan's wealthy uncle suddenly appeared in haste and febrile desperation, bringing with him his favorite chair to camp beneath the protective arch over their huge fireplace. He refused to budge for days, petrified by his fear of bombs that never fell. In the meantime, he expected Cornelia to bring his food to him, while he hatched impossible plans to escape to his houses in Spain and North Africa. His presence made everyone rather nervous.

Willem adapted. He was fiercely anti-government, anti-Calvinist, and anti-Catholic. This was perhaps his natural rebellion against the religious authority that had trampled indiscriminately all over the fertile garden of his childhood sensitivities.

Another ingredient adding to Willem's hardening pro-German position was his accumulation of so much medical experience with the lower classes of society. His egalitarian ambitions for social medicine aligned themselves with anything new that might break down the old, crystallized institutions. He was, after all, a man of paradox. As a member of the NSB (the National Socialist movement), he volunteered for the indoctrination camps, where he mixed with the party regulars and leaders. This was the highly unpopular pro-German group running the Dutch administration under German direction. But as Willem's German connection waxed, so he became more and more ostracized by his community, his income waning to next to nothing.

Jan continued to ride along the shore, now punctuated with numerous forbidding bunkers facing seawards.

Occasionally, a German officer would canter alongside. They were polite, even affable, in the correct Prussian military manner—and fine horsemen. The officer's own sense of loyalty made him feel awkward when his comrades told him how much they missed their children back in the Fatherland.

Poverty forced the family to move to Amsterdam, where Willem had been offered a post in the Health Department. Jan and Machteld went to the high school serving the children of the NSB, together with those of the German officers. He had no friends except Machteld, who always shared Jan's fate and was his only source of emotional support. He had trouble with the languge, and they had to walk a long way to school. They were always cold and hungry. The taunts and sneering rejection by Jan's peers only compounded his misery. He found himself an outcast in his own country: "Your dad is a traitor! You go to a German school! You are not one of us! You don't belong here!"

The goose-stepping German eagles became a common sight on Jan's way to school. Jan gave the secret police headquarters a wide berth. Passing the guards several times on the other side of the street, he had observed the dark-windowed cars pull up at the entrance. An occasional muffled cry from within gave the whole place an ominous aura—it was a good place to avoid. Jan was surprised to see people wearing the Star of David on their chests appearing in the streets. He knew that his father had been sympathetic to them in the past, indeed, many of his psychiatric colleagues were Jews. It was another of Willem's ambivalences.

Jan became a member of a youth group affiliated with the Hitler youth movement and was given a drum to practice on, which drove his parents crazy. The group leaders organized a scheme to send groups of urban youth to the villages and resort camps in southern Germany to support the war effort and learn something about country life. Jan's group, which included his sister, left by train. Their destination was tranquility itself, but the journey was the opposite—a nightmare. The train scurried through several Ruhr stations, turned into blazing infernos by night raids, while the sky was interlaced with probing searchlights and shell bursts. They ran a gauntlet of detonations, the shock waves hurling everyone onto the floor in heaps of panic. The train swayed and lurched at speed, only to stop like a sacrificial lamb on the altar rails for what seemed like an eternity, before being shunted on to new lines. No one seemed to be in charge; no one knew what was going on—but Jan and Machteld got through unscathed.

While lodged with a German farming family, Jan fed the cows and pigs and threw some hay around, but he was not really involved. Feeling very much alone, his suspicion prevented him from making friends. Of course, Jan had his usual problems with the language, especially the southern German dialect. Country life was primitive. The toilet was a hole cut in an upstairs wall. You had to sit on the edge and listen to the sloppy thud of excreta on the manure pile three floors below—the stench was asphyxiating. All Jan wanted to do was eat. The dark bread he liked so much helped increase his weight to the point where Willem later placed him on a starvation regimen, forcing Jan to run every day until he could keep up with Machteld.

Willem left for Poland and the Ukraine to assist the colonization program to Germanize the eastern areas of the country, but nothing went right and he was soon bitterly disillusioned. The more he saw, the greater grew the chill of Willem's dismay. He had always felt empathy for the peasants and was incensed by the way they were brutalized and exploited by the "Master Race." Willem could never talk to his children about his duties and the anguish he felt; he was not a man to reveal his guilt.

Willem felt compelled to leave, but he dared not return to the hostility in Holland. After considerable inquiries and applications, he was offered a medical position in southern Germany. So the family moved to a tiny village near Stuttgart.

Jan attended the Johann Kepler High School where, as usual, he did not fit in. At least Jan recognized one theme common to his first history lessons in his last three schools. Apparently, the Germans had appropriated Caesar's claim—Veni Vidi Vici. Regarded as a foreigner, Jan was neither accepted nor rejected, but he was relieved to be free from the dark hostility he'd felt in Holland. He enjoyed racing his sister to school, cycling up and down the hills; and he liked the quiet villagers who often brought milk and fruit to his family. He felt at ease with the simple routines of rural life.

Despite the sedate environment, however, the village was not oblivious to the war. Many a tense night was spent in a cramped cellar, while one sinister phalanx of bombers after another droned overhead to pulverize the industrial guts of the Reich. Obviously, the situation was worsening since the beleaguered heavens now raged in conflict by day and by night.

They were not the only displaced persons in the area. Across the street was a camp of foreign factory workers from Poland and Russia. They were a taciturn, surly, and roughly dressed bunch. Jan himself occasionally worked in a factory, helping to assemble pumps for military equipment. The manager, who had given Jan a room in his house, encouraged him to spend his free time in the workshops. Jan was delighted to discover how things functioned and marveled at the ingenuity of it all. He even began to read blueprints, thus demonstrating a certain inherent talent in this respect.

The family radio continued boasting about the success of the U-boats sinking yet another massive tonnage of Allied merchantships. But Dr. Goebbels's propaganda mill was rapidly running out of excuses and reasonable disinformation. The family did hear about the catastrophic loss of Stalingrad and the collapsing eastern front. These setbacks had a devastating effect on the people's morale.

Cornelia, at this time, seemed to sleep most of the day, sunk in depression. It was Jan's sister, his beloved co-victim, who ran the household. Jan had lost contact with his mother; no one really confided in anyone, and for him home was nothing more than a malaise of silence or quarreling. Cornelia suffered a miscarriage. Jan heard the screams and saw blood, but he had no idea what was going on. Like so many of the children of turmoil, war did not permit Jan to stumble his way through the troublesome but essential threshold of adolescence. A floundering childhood, followed by the tumult of war, telescoped Jan's natural passage to maturity. Instead of trailing clouds of glory, happily sauntering through his seasons of awakening, he was roughly frog-marched into prematurity. Jan's growing years were deprived of the warmth, humor, play, and understanding of adult love-filled interaction. All he felt was the hard-edged hand of adult dubiety. His adolescence vanished into thin air, barring him from fantastic flights with the eagles of intellect, the blushes of romance, the stirrings of ideals. Not permitted to paddle, then wade gently into the river of age, he was thrown into its wildest rapids. The philosophy he met was that of survival; history and geography he was condemned to suffer firsthand and experience as bitter reality. It would take a lifetime to overcome Jan's almost permanent state of puberty.

The Germans, in a desperate last-ditch effort to stem the enemy advance, recruited hordes of gangly seniors from the high schools. Jan listened to the patriotic, hysterical clichés thundering around the auditorium: "Fight to protect your Fatherland, your Eastern heritage, your family! Germany needs you!" So Jan, like the others, "volunteered" for basic training in a Waffen SS camp. The elite SS had several international brigades made up of Norwegians, Dutch, Yugoslavians, Italians, and so on. Jan was seventeen when he joined other Dutch youngsters in the rigors of boot camp. There were night marches, hours of meticulous scrubbing and cleaning, maneuvers with live ammunition, obstacle courses, test after test of endurance under the remorseless drill sergeants. The army mentality expunged all traces of independence and turned them into corporate instruments of conflict. When they were deemed ready for combat, suitable cannon fodder for the Reich marshals, they were recklessly shoved in front of Patton's pugnacious Fifth Army.

Jan's unit was sent straight to the front. His officers had noticed Jan's innate sense of direction, and he was given the highly dangerous work of being a courier. Communication between the command posts and the forward positions is particularly primitive when an army is in retreat. The rearguard action was fierce and the disintegrating units fought bravely, but Patton's relentless onslaught thrust them ever backwards. Tired and disheveled, hungry and scared, Jan spent his days and nights scrambling along water-logged ditches, darting from crater to crater, crawling through exposed meadows, bent double behind tottering walls, or picking his way through woods, while a variety of violence shredded the foliage above his helmet. The military telephone service was highly unreliable, even comical in such conditions, and the couriers were immensely valuable—if they survived.

Jan bitterly resented the fact that the other men refused to take the risk. He never once used his rifle since he was always scrambling, stooping below that butchering zone of whistling shells and bullets. The headquarters were mostly located in the cellars of demolished buildings. No one there seemed to have an overall picture of the military situation, which changed from minute to minute. Jan saw plenty of helplessly frightened officers clearly not in command of anyone, not even themselves. As the confusion mounted, so the morale plummeted. He saw officers running for their lives, deserting their men to fend for themselves; indeed, on Jan's daily sorties he would encounter retreating and demoralized officers together with men, guns, and tanks in total disarray. Everyone made for the Rhine, Jan's unit being one of those sacrificed to hold the deteriorating lines while the others escaped. The retreating troops blew up the Rhine bridges, leaving the rearguard units stranded under fierce bombardment from both friend and foe. Jan ducked, crawled, flattened himself, and scurried in a fixed seizure of anxiety, surviving on his razor-sharp instinct powered by adrenaline.

Under the dubious cover of darkness, confounded by an occasional star shell, during a lull in the barrage the remnants of Jan's unit crossed the dark, swiftly moving river in small boats. It was ominously quiet except for the muffled oars. They paddled, heads lowered, minds riveted on the distant shore somewhere in the blackness beyond. They crossed their Lethe safely and were taken behind the lines to receive medical treatment and food. Easing his badly blistered feet into warm water was sheer bliss.

Jan was soon sent to a base in southern Germany to retrain, regroup, and be placed in a fresh division. Ordered to the eastern front, his unit went by train but really had no idea of their final destination. Later on Jan learned that they had passed through Austria and into Hungary to be stationed near Lake Balaton, as part of a massive concentration of men and material. The intense press of soldiers and total lack of privacy aroused his claustrophobia again. Like so many, he suffered from the debilitating, not to mention embarrassing, effects of diarrhea. His anguish forced him to volunteer for an outpost on the forward line, facing the unstoppable Soviet steamroller.

The ludicrous confusion here was worse than that of the western front. This was a milling morass of retreating men and machines. Time and time again Jan had to help free vehicles trapped by the viscous mud and wet snow of the spring thaw. The roads were jammed with soldiers and vehicles trapped in the desperate tide of fleeing refugees. There were thousands of them, the old and the infirm, the women with children perched on their shoulders dragging their handfuls of pitiful belongings away from the Russians. He could see them being rudely shoved into the ditches to make room for the tanks, and the terror surged every time the roads were indiscriminately strafed by the low-flying Russian aircraft. The loss of life was devastating, and the wounded lay unattended. These maniacal images would be burnt in permanent white on the black despondence of Jan's memory.

The fields of mud were filled with people trying to shelter under makeshift tents made from blankets. The front lines were impossible to define, and the suffocating chaos rendered all maps utterly useless, while the crescendo of the Russian artillery barrage increased by the hour. Jan wondered where the real fighting was taking place in this huge theater of confusion. Where was the man-to-man combat? There were no enemy eyes to look upon in this atmospheric storm of shells and bombs, bullets and rockets. Jan was still a courier, now based in a derelict house together with a dozen comrades, one of them being a young Dutchman like himself. This dispirited group waited for transport to be taken back to the main group.

Everyone now realized that nothing could block the Russian onslaught—they knew the war was lost. Rumors of a superbomb developed by the Allies had percolated through to the troops. The Führer had promised them he would unleash such a weapon to bring his enemies to their knees. Now it was too late. Now it was every man for himself. They knew the immediate future was either death or the icy solitude of a Siberian prison camp and wondered why they should stay at their posts while all around them they saw officers in full flight.

The truck arrived on a bitterly chilled, moonlit night. The Germans scrambled aboard, but Jan and Pete hid in the trees nearby. After a few calls, the truck left without them and the night fell silent. Jan felt swallowed up by guilt, the first emotion other than fear to swamp him in a long time. He had deserted his comrades, comrades who had always protected and covered for each other. He remembered sharing his very first cognac with them, a dusty bottle discovered while sheltering in the cellar of a demolished house near the front. This guilt was the most nauseating emotion in Jan's war, and the feeling of acidic shame and self-revulsion would never leave him.

They set out westwards, away from the Russians, travelling in uniform with their rifles on their shoulders, knowing that if they were caught, they would be shot. Sometimes they jumped into the backs of trucks slowing to change gears before climbing the hills. Occasionally they sheltered in the barns of terrified Hungarian farmers. The trucks stopped at checkpoints from time to time, and Jan and Pete held their breath, dreading the thrust of the bayonet into the interior darkness of their safety. It was almost a circadian rhythm of holding their breath, then releasing their relief. When questioned, they said they were returning to boot camp.

Soon they were south of Vienna, moving ever westward following the Inn River. They were stopped again, but this time they were driven to Mauthausen concentration camp for further questioning. Both had to recite their fabricated stories to the commandant of the camp—an SS man. Jan felt totally helpless; he had never faced such a frightening presence—he was absolutely petrified. In the meantime, Jan and Pete both worked in the kitchen, peeling potatoes. At least it was warm and they had a plentiful supply of food, not like the other poor devils behind the wire. This was the first time Jan had seen the wraithlike creatures: groups of shuffling pallor and stiffened bones, striped caricatures of human beings trapped in the suffocating gloom. He could never exorcise this hellish vision of human desecration—and he would never understand it.

Pete was a tall, blond, handsome fellow whose easygoing charm made him popular with the ladies. He somehow managed to flirt with one of the camp secretaries, lovingly persuading her to falsify their papers so they could leave. Through Pete, Jan also made friends with one of them; indeed, it was in this very trough of human despair and deprivation that he blundered into his first sexual experience. It was a single, furtively short-lived flurry of sensation, which left Jan's natural longing abashed and guilty. They nevertheless got their faked papers and were allowed to go on their way, after being in Mauthausen for two weeks.

The pair continued to follow the river, which led them through many Austrian villages where at least they could now comprehend the language. The valleys grew steeper, the mountains higher, as they moved closer to the Swiss border, where they hoped to intercept the American troops pressing northward through Italy. The sound of distant gunfire spurred them on. They managed to hitchhike a ride on a train close to Salzburg. It was a beautiful, cloudless spring day. About midday, however, the train was suddenly engulfed by terror when the sky rained ribbons of bombs down on them. Their train screeched to a halt, with the station less than half a mile away. Everyone scrambled out to take cover below the embankment. While the earth thundered and heaved in its agony, the dust, debris, fumes, and smoke choked both body and soul. When the paroxysm cleared, they saw that the station ahead was nothing but a heap of rubble.

Jan and Pete climbed farther into the mountains while the increasing sounds of battle indicated the noisy proximity of the American advance. High above the snow line they came across a shepherd's hut, complete with a store of useful peasant clothes. After changing, they dumped their uniforms and began a careful descent. Shells passed over their heads, while several hundred feet below a bridge was being blown up by the retreating Germans. The American tanks were pinned down on the other side.

From their cover, Jan and Pete watched the engineers constructing a pontoon bridge. Seeing the tanks begin to move, they knew it was time to throw away their rifles and make their way down towards the vanguard of the American forces. Like thousands of other displaced fugitives of war, they would try to pass themselves off as civilians.

After picking their way down the wooded slopes to the road, they met the vanguard units—who completely ignored them. No one showed the slightest interest in them until, further on, they were questioned by support troops, who then escorted them to a makeshift refugee camp. All around them milled the flotsam and jetsam of war, a motley assemblage of foreign workers, peasants caught in the wrong place at the wrong time, deserters mingling in hope of obscurity, and some utterly wretched-looking survivors from the concentration camps. The mood in the camp was one of relief or apprehension, depending on whose eyes Jan looked into.

Jan and Pete were appointed bunks, given food, and told to wait for their names to be called. Jan, at least, had one remarkable advantage—all SS troops had their blood group tattooed on one arm. Like everyone else, he had lined up in the boot camp to have it inscribed, but a surprise bombing raid disrupted the proceedings and Jan left for the front soon afterwards—without the revelatory stigma. He did, however, see the telltale blood types on other arms, together with those identifying the obvious ghostlike remnants of the death camps.

Caught in the brooding zone between fate and freedom, Jan waited for hours, sitting, standing, prowling restlessly around the perimeter wire, anxious about his approaching interrogation. The inevitable moment arrived and he was led into a small, barely furnished room, containing a table, a stenographer, and a lone American intelligence officer. The procedure, though agonizing, was quite different to his fearful confrontation at Mauthausen, where the approach was to bluster, intimidate, and abuse.

The immaculate, fresh-faced officer smiled, offered Jan a cigarette, and appeared friendly, relaxed, and low key. But Jan lowered his mental portcullis; his opponent was the adversary holding all the power. The officer probed in a matter-of-fact way, seeming to be rather considerate and easygoing. But then, luring Jan into a false sense of security, he would relax the pressure to pursue a new path of questioning, only to abruptly switch to a previously pivotal sticking point—always checking and rechecking. "Where did you say you got those papers? Who gave them to you? How did you learn to read blueprints? What were you doing in Germany? Tell me about your family. I thought you said you were . . ."

It was a devious game—one as deadly as Russian roulette. One false move, one crack in Jan's edifice of lies, and he was doomed by being unmasked as one of the enemy. Jan imagined himself being executed, but there is nothing like being poised on the razor-edge of survival to concentrate the mind. His adrenaline-heightened wits were quick and sharp—his speech slow and deliberate. He stuck to his story, venturing nothing, saying as little as possible. When presented with a way out, he refused to play along. Jan lived by his mental agility from second to second—each second of delay enabled him to think before answering—his mind instinctively geared to its survival mode. First the SS at Mauthausen, and now the Americans, threatened to strip him of his cover. Afterwards, he slept fitfully in the barracks, waiting to be called by day or by night. Was each episode merely another nail in his coffin? He wondered if he could withstand the stress. Did they believe him?

Without warning, he was transferred to a much larger camp at Annecy in France, a place enclosed by lakes and beautiful scenery. Jan remembered that his father had once vacationed in this lovely area. Here he made sure he kept to himself and did not confide in anyone. He had lost all contact with his friend Pete. As far as he was concerned, no one could be trusted. Yet Jan's craving for human warmth lowered his shield when an older man offered him some precious kindness and attention. Their stroll in a meadow behind the camp led to Jan's only homosexual experience, which inflicted yet another wound of guilt on his psyche and innocence.

The interviews became even more psychologically manipulating. The skill of the interrogators was definitely superior to those Jan had previously confounded. In one session he was asked to pronounce certain Dutch words unique to the mother tongue—to prove his heritage. At least one thing in his youth favored Jan, all those mortifying interrogations by his father had prepared him well.

Again, without warning, Jan was led to the interrogation room. This time, however, he was handed some official documents, told to return to Holland, and curtly dismissed. It took his well-buried heart a moment or two to uncork its euphoria. He was free! The game was over. At last, he was free!

A few hours later, Jan stepped upon Dutch soil for the first time in four years. Then the sobering realization struck him; he was a stranger in his own land—just one more refugee of war. Having no idea of the whereabouts of his parents, Jan decided, in desperation, to visit his aunt and uncle in Laren, a village south of Amsterdam. Their greeting registered both surprise and a tremor of apprehension. Knowing full well Jan's Nazi past, they were well apprised of the danger of protecting him. He stayed with them for four months, mostly confined to the basement during the daylight hours, since the Dutch police net was still trawling the streets for Nazi sympathizers. Jan did venture out after dark from time to time, but he kept to the shadows and side streets. But this was an unhealthy confinement for an already disoriented twenty year old, and it resulted in a spasmodic love affair with his aunt, who was only a year or two older than he.

Margot was an energetic, attractive woman whose weekly dinner parties were both popular and alcoholically boisterous. She ran the pharmacy for her doctor husband, a man of portly dimensions, mostly preoccupied with his practice and alcohol. The affair was more of an ephemeral amusement, a mutual titillation, while uncle was oblivious to the extracurricular activities in his bedroom. For Jan, it was nothing more than a slight infatuation, something to remove the boredom—an unexpected boon of sensation and stimulation. There was nothing serious about it, except being yet another episode adding more grist to the mill of his conscience.

Jan decided he wanted to attend the technical university in Delft. His uncle helped Jan approach his grandfather, who placed some funds at Jan's disposal. Jan signed a contract stating he had no past connection to the Nazis. The classes were enormous, typical of the European schools at that time with so many teachers dead, injured, or in process of being demobilized. The sheer size of the student body precluded any personal contact with the professors. Of course, Jan still kept to himself, not daring to expose his German past, but he did join a fraternity. To do this he had to suffer the inevitable initiation practices, harrowing, cruel, and humiliating as they were. Terrified by this "hazing" as they called it, Jan could not express his fear to anyone. So with tremor in the pit of his stomach, aware of his hammering heartbeat, he suffered throughout, while being hosed and covered with beer, then running the gauntlet of violent books and towels. The fraternity symbol was the rising phoenix; Jan hoped it would symbolize his own fortunes.

Being a member of the rowing fraternity helped Jan relax. He was comfortable with this kind of discipline, order, and steadiness, glad to be away from the drinking parties, those cliques of spoiled youth from the upperclass families. Rowing helped to rebuild him physically and mentally, and he enjoyed the rhythmic effort, the physical challenge, and the camaraderie engendered through teamwork. Jan loved being on the water in the early morning freshness. Of course, he had to attend the noisy drinking parties after the competitions, but mostly he kept to himself.

Then, as if fate chose to exact a penalty for Jan's unaccustomed peace of mind, he was rudely arrested by the regular Dutch police and taken straightway to the infamous Scheveningen prison close to Haarlem. Many a Dutch patriot had been tortured and killed by the gestapo in this forbidding institution, not to mention the Jews who met their end there. Later on Jan learned that a member of his own family had betrayed him. One of his aunts had recently married a Jewish lawyer, who had survived Hitler's "final solution." It was his hypersensitive suspicion and demand for justice that demolished Jan's fledgling feeling of safety.

Again, the interrogation drama unfolded, again Jan resurrected his story and held onto it. By now his tale was so defined and tested under fire, he half believed it himself. He was locked in his impasse: they could not break him and Jan failed to convince them. Two of Jan's fraternity friends labored for hours to persuade him to let go and reveal the truth, confident that the authorities would not be too hard on him when they knew all the facts. After hours of resistance, Jan threw open the doors of his stockade by narrating the complete unamended version of his past. Now he was no longer compelled to hide, fudge, and lie—and it worked. Jan's private war was over; the Dutch intelligence let him go. But was he really free? Could he go and do as he pleased? He was twenty years old and had crammed a dozen lifetimes in that period. Forbidden by the authorities to return to the university in Delft, Jan looked elsewhere, but the only option open to reason was to rejoin his family.

Willem had been dragged through his own litany of prison-camp interrogations, following his arrest by French troops. While he was incarcerated, Cornelia had struggled valiantly to protect the family from the dismaying postwar poverty and insecurity. After his release, Willem opened a new practice, south of Rotterdam, where the family settled into a small house and the children returned to school. Jan felt acute discomfort as soon as he arrived. He was happy to see Machteld again after so long, but everyone seemed to be on edge. There was not enough affection to keep any avenues of communication open. Everyone talked at the other, not to them. Jan felt like an intruder; to make matters worse, he had no job or educational prospects, which made him frustratingly dependent on his father.

Then the papers arrived commanding Jan to report as a conscript to a Dutch army camp for training. This appalling news confirmed for Jan that the fateful hound that had shaken him for so long, still refused to unclamp its jaws. He was devastated. Anything with a military connotation filled Jan with sheer dread and revulsion, yet soon he would be back in boot camp. For a moment he considered making yet another flight to freedom; he had done it before, he could do it again. This time, however, his trusty instinct could not ignite his will. Jan had lost his drive and felt overwhelmingly defeated.

Jan did as he was told, hoping to sink into complete anonymity—but to no avail. His comrades wondered about his obvious sharp-shooting skills and inquired about his seemingly natural ability in handling all the duties, exercises, and military paraphernalia. Of course, Jan could not confide in them. Not daring to expose his past, he concocted yet another story, another pack of lies. He became an automaton—going through his military motions—a robotic twenty year old.

By now his inundated psyche was at saturation point. One day Jan simply walked away from the barracks, past the guard posts, and along the dikes. Oblivious to caution, his torpid mind disengaged from the rational world of cause and effect; it was his way of slipping away from his aching reality. He returned a few hours later, in his own good time, to face a serious misdemeanor charge before being placed in confinement then hammered by another battery of interrogators. After his anxious parents contacted the commander of the camp, Jan was scrupulously examined by a camp doctor, who promptly referred him to a military psychiatric hospital equipped to handle war traumas of those exiled from wholeness and balance.

Jan, now twenty-one years old, would be a resident here for one and a half years. This neurosis hospital was no prison; there were no guards or barricades. The psychiatrists and nurses were friendly, responsive people, and the minimal rules were designed to be simple and considerate. There was plenty of time for exercise and group therapy sessions, reading, hypnosis, psychodrama, and sensitive communication. The residential houses were spaced well apart, and the inmates had plenty of leisure time to ramble around the spacious, well-cared-for grounds. This was where fractured psyches, dismembered by the shattering intrusions of war, could be healed through time, caring, and sharing. In such a place the psyche could begin to absorb and assimilate its crushing burden of pain; guilt and terror could be gently faced. It was a place where the crumbled self might reassemble and reconstitute itself—a sanctuary where the future became a conceivable possibility.

The days were relaxed and gently structured. Some residents appeared to be rather normal; a few shook with nervous spasms, even convulsions, from time to time; others reacted with terror to the slightest noise; while a few poor souls remained suspended, transfixed in their catatonic seclusion. But the nights were restless and uneasy. Under cover of darkness, demons escaped from their subterranean hideouts, hurling memories about the rooms, splitting the quiet with the screams of nightmare, then subsiding into sobs, shivers, and sweats. Thank God for those good sentinels always ready to render the comfort of a light, a soothing word, a touch, wiping the beaded brow—and the grim spectres would retreat for a while.

This oasis of human reconstruction was itself a perpetuation of war, the conflict now raging within individual psyches. Many there had been torn apart on the rack stretched between the imperative instincts of survival and their deeply set duty to comrades sharing the heat of battle. The aftermath left many bereft of self-cohesion, psychic unity. The psyche, under intense assault, had lost the control of its authentic self. There were legions of the dispossessed, stripped of the centrality of the ego. It was a daunting challenge, indeed, to put Humpty Dumpty together again. For many it would take a lifetime. Slowly the lengthy process of restoration began to reassemble the fragments of Jan's battered psyche and rekindle the flame of his will. Dominated by the urge to choose and then master his own destiny, Jan was determined never again to submit to the tyranny of others. There had to be a way to assume full control of his life to come. Of course, his past was not all guilt and storm. There were a few useful seeds scattered about in the continuum of his years waiting for the proper soil and season to germinate. They were planted as long ago as Jan's infancy in the asylum and as recently as his camp and hospital experience.

Jan now felt more at ease in the daily discussions, finding that he could actually override his defense mechanisms and reveal his deeper feelings. He had many thought-provoking talks with the doctors about the nature and future of psychiatry and medicine. All around him were shattered men like himself, the slowly mending souls of pilots, sailors, privates, and officers. Jan felt part of this genesis of hope, this brotherhood of pain, and he began to think seriously about medicine as a possible career. This would be a way he could assist others, especially the casualties of war. Could he really become a healer? Jan wondered. Perhaps it was the same for doctors as artists, if Nietzsche was right when he suggested that the artist speaks through the mouth of his wound. Perhaps only those who had suffered could truly heal.

Eighteen months after his arrival, Jan was released. Realizing he would have to begin at the very bottom, he took several high-school crash courses in Rotterdam. After a few months, he was accepted by Leiden University, fully primed to invest all his resurgent will into years of medical study. Becoming a highly tuned machine capable of absorbing massive loads of information, Jan resisted going to parties and sacrificed his vacations. All that mattered now was his remorseless climb towards opportunity. To succeed in his plans, Jan was determined to achieve five years of medical study in three years. Although his SS cloud still hovered about him, nothing mattered now except his freedom to prepare a career and disconnect himself once and for all from his parents.

Then he met Maryke. She was introduced to him by a cousin, following a gathering of women students at the university. Jan, whose highly neglected though passionate emotional nature made him a prime candidate for a fervid romance, was soon captivated by her quick intelligence and petite, though robust, feminine form. Maryke had blondish hair, blue eyes, and carried herself with a natural poise and elegance. Jan was drawn to her subtle softness, the special feminine mellowness indicative of Indonesian women. Maryke's vitality and humor brought a lightness, a breath of refreshing rapture into the stoic studiousness dominating Jan's days and nights. Maryke had studied art in The Hague, and in Jan's eyes, her artistic sensibilities added even more luster to her feminine charm. He also admired her strength of spirit, surprisingly evident in the way she stood up to his father's petulance. Maryke in turn was drawn to Jan's youthfulness, his vigorous love of action. Like many thrust prematurely out of the Eden of childhood, Jan had preserved a certain boyishness and engaging charm. Maryke also admired his total commitment to study; she had always been attracted to strong masculinity.

Yet theirs was a match made in adversity, since Maryke also carried with her a turbulent and painful history. Before the war, her father had been a Dutch commissioner in Indonesia, responsible for supervising the local governments of several wide-spread territories. He was away much of the time and Maryke suffered from protracted periods of loneliness and boredom—her playmates being many days distant. Later, during the Japanese occupation, Maryke had been interned with her mother in one of the notorious concentration camps in Java. Many of her formative years were spent in the company of women thrown together in the squalor and privation of these tropical hell holes. Here Maryke was exposed to those most remarkable women who fought so stubbornly to protect the children from life-threatening hazards of the primitive conditions, not to mention the brutal intimidation of their Japanese masters. The essentially male-centered mentality of the Japanese psyche was incapable of understanding these indomitable European women, and was daily confounded by their sheer resourcefulness and determination. These petticoat brigades survived by strict organization and by pooling their considerable talents.

Maryke, therefore, had mostly feminine role models and had been exposed to the incredibly resilient survival instincts of the maternal spirit. She could recognize Jan's interior strength developed through similar circumstances. Similarly, both had parts of themselves that were totally neglected, and both of them had blocked themselves off from their deep reservoirs of anger.

Maryke and Jan were married in the courthouse a month before the birth of their first child. Jan was twenty-six; Maryke was twenty-four. They lived in an unheated garret near the university. It was a damp and musty tenement in an old building. To reach it they had to climb a poorly lit spiral staircase up three floors. The newlyweds took great pains not to alienate their rather prickly landlady, a dragonlike character who detested little children. Here Maryke struggled through the first experiments of motherhood, trying to keep the baby warm despite frozen-stiff diapers and little money. Jan studied as best he could at a small kitchen table, to the accompaniment of his often crying son, Diaz.

Money was always their foremost source of anxiety. Willem's support payments were absolutely crucial. He was particularly unpredictable at this time, while struggling to rebuild his family and recover his professional standing. For the sake of survival Jan had to make every effort to be passive and agreeable; he dared not do or say anything that might jeopardize the precious allowance. One moment his father was light and friendly, the next, fractious and accusative. Jan hated the pretense, but it made him work all the harder.

Jan's sister, Machteld, married against the wishes of Willem and Cornelia thus precipitating a major family crisis. Jan invited his father's wrath by deciding to attend the forbidden ceremony. Willem promptly stopped the allowance, which caused them acute distress for two months. To make matters worse, Maryke had her own familial troubles. She had neglected to tell her father, still in Indonesia, that she was married. These mutual family antagonisms and the lamentable living conditions brought them closer together. Their occasional flare-ups, to be expected from two such willful and stubborn individuals, did little to hamper their loving devotion to each other. Whenever possible, the fledgling family enjoyed their outings. Sometimes Jan would fasten his highly cocooned infant on the back of his bicycle and ride around the parks;

also the family sailed on Kaag lake close to Leiden, in the relieving spring sunshine.

The love between Maryke and Jan, warmed by their first real experience of sexual and family intimacy and the feeling of "us against the hostile world," overrode Jan's flawed perception of woman. As a youth, he had tried to support his mother only to suffer recrimination and betrayal. Thus, his impressionable years were dominated by his father and men like him, whereas his primary feminine role model lacked any real consistency. Willem, with his own chaotic sexuality, viewed all relationships through Freudian-tinted spectacles. He blasted Jan's natural caring mercilessly, always unmasking it as an Oedipal form of behavior. Willem always regarded Jan as his rival, which in turn stifled Jan's own feminine side, leaving him with an emotional handicap that would cause him no end of trouble later on.

As Jan neared his graduation, he seriously began to consider leaving Holland and taking his family westward to America, away from the aggravating proximity of his parents and the inhibiting stigma of his past.

* * *

I am Chronos and I shall instruct you. Let it be known to you that every self prepares, then endures, its self-chosen destiny. Take heed! Hear the irrepressible call of an evolution resounding through every region of our universe—"Human, experience thyself!"

Know also that civilizations, nations, and societies emerge and subside according to the appointed rhythms of change. Uphold the thought that your personal destiny is meshed with the wider sweeps of the global cycles; your life is inconceivable without your suspension in the social milieu. Thus there are times when the personal may be inundated, submerged, and obscured by the pressure of the transpersonal—but it is never lost. Realize this, there are countless mansions of purpose and meaning unknown to you. Ranged above are worlds that receive your every thought and action. You live for yourself but never for yourself alone.

Through its incessant drive, this universe spirals to ever-higher octaves of being. Likewise, your earth lifts itself on the wings of experience to higher regions of its own self-perception. Thus does this universe advance and enlarge its own identity. I am but the servant of this ascendance and you are my religion: you *are* the religion of the living cosmos. So does your destiny, the handmaiden of Cosmic Love, sanctify your existence.

I am Chronos! My name among the Romans was "Saturn," and the planet bearing my name circles its sun orbit in thirty years. This very beat is my foundation cycle, inscribed within every mortal life span.

Remember well! Your thirtieth and sixtieth years, together with the median points at fifteen and forty-five, are likely to be marked by major events, situations, precipitating a change in direction, a change of emphasis. There may well be urgent predicaments for you at such times, since they are the turning points on your paths, pivotal changes that may well construct a crisis.

Be not afeared of your *crises*. The word stems from the Greek "to decide." Despite possible disorientation, suffering, upheaval, and unexpected intrusions, rejoice! They do but inform you! The gifts within them offer you the gold of opportunity, confirming the truth that you are ALIVE. You are in movement. You are casting off your past as you move through the threshold of transformation and renewal. Yes, rejoice in them and acclaim them though they may blast you from your status quo when the psyche demands action. Only time will disclose the meaning, the virtues hidden within them.

I am Chronos-Saturn and my major cycles reign from birth to thirty, from thirty to sixty, from sixty to ninety. May the first of my rhythms be named the Preparatory Cycle. It is here, in your first thirty years, that you engage those formative influences that shape your future. Here you assimilate your heredity and social nutriments. Here life bestows on you countless blessings and even those perilous resistances, the seeds that will fructify in the seasons of your future time. I tell you, you would not have them if you had no need of them later on.

Mark well! Each increment of your genesis is placed into its proper position by the sway of your rhythms. Without the cyclic beat of the heart, you would not know life. Without the rhythms of your psyche, you would be without order, and the purpose resident in you could not unfold. Without my order, you would be crushed by the sheer mass of uncoordinated experience. As you digest your bread, so you digest your events to become who you are—the Self your aspiring, though subterranean reality, seeks to become.

Know this! Only when you scan the whole will you intuit how each blessing, each hammer blow on the anvil of your unique self, shapes the metal of your emerging being. Fear not the pain. All suffering, when transmuted by the alchemy of the self, when overcome, becomes the eye that penetrates the mysteries of life, that knows.

I am Chronos-Saturn and I will preview your future spans. In your time between birth and thirty you have gathered a vast and complex array of indispensable experience. By thirty, you have shaped the wondrous essence of your destiny, centered in the core of your uniqueness.

You are ready; you are prepared and poised to go forth on your quest.

This first cycle is likely to be concluded by a transition, a possible crisis which can appear in many guises, a special *journey*, or a *conflict*, perhaps even an illness compelling you to jettison your past.

In the cycle between thirty and sixty you pour your talents, gifts, weaknesses, ideas, and ideals into the very chalice of life, and the reflection of your interaction with the world will generate your evolving relationship to yourself and your world. Let this be known as the Constructive Cycle.

My closing cycle from sixty to death will be a span of completion and disengagement, a Reflective Cycle in which your past is absorbed and digested, to be incorporated into the very essence of who you are. Standing on the higher escarpments of your time, your life wisdom shall bring guidance and blessing to those wending their way along the lower footpaths. Although you may appear to harden into rigidity and resistance to change, all you have gathered from the abundant fields of your time, will amalgamate with your being. All this you must carry as the essence, the seedcorn passing beyond your mortal dissolution. Breathing is the universal image of all life. In your opening cycle you inhale the formative ingredients of your experience. In your second cycle you breathe yourself into the world. At sixty, you inhale the previous cycle into the metabolic dynamics of your psyche until the threshold of death, when you exhale the eternal essence of yourself into those unfathomable dimensions of your immortality.

I am Chronos. Do not fear me. I am the husbandman of your transit, arranging the cycles that draw your life to its fruition. I am empowered by those high beings who invest the worlds becoming with the ever-transformative force of love. Remember my law: As you sow the seeds of action so shall you reap the harvest of future experience and eventual self-knowing. Your path shall be from "Human know thyself" to "Human love thyself." It is as fundamental, as painful, and as mysterious as that.

Look now upon Jan's formative span and mark well the key motives orchestrated to echo throughout his later passage. These are the motives I shall signpost: the interplay of diverse peoples; the struggle against rigidity, authority, and control; his submergence in conflict and hostility; the warring of people close to him and nations around him; his love of the sea—his metaphor for freedom; his seedling interests in medicine, psychiatry, and construction. All these ingredients will continue to reverberate throughout his life to come.

Consider also the psychological effects and tendencies wrought in Jan's early life—its pervasive insecurity, emotional deprivation, and guilt. You may be tempted to call them "damages," but I shall define them as *resistances* to be challenged and overcome for future growth.

Mark well his instinctive reactions, his compulsive drive to sever himself from the pain-ridden levels of his vulnerability. Adversity had built the strength of a will compelled to seek goal after goal in a desperate search for self-vindication and social acceptance. Jan's denial abandoned whole regions of his vulnerability, but this, the devotional, venerational, intuitive roots of his emotional reality, will never abandon him. They will exert their ruthless influence on his cycles to come and curse his relations with women.

Mark well that the natural survival instincts of Jan's early years would harden into the compulsive and stubborn patterns he would adopt time and time again. The psyche, however, is empowered to grow, and it cannot do so if trapped in emotional straitjackets. These old patterns will cramp Jan's coming years and produce crisis after crisis. His escapes only serve to drive him deeper into the thicket of confusion.

Will you render moral judgement? I shall not, but you are human and you are he, he is you. No matter. But hold firm the truth that nothing here diminishes the quest of a soul in search of itself. The plain truth within this tale is Jan's chase for his uniqueness through the perilous terrain of earthly experience.

Before we continue, mark well his turning-point at fifteen—when the tides of war engulfed him. Note, too, his epochal decision to move westward, a journey he will make when he is thirty. And so it is.

South Africa, Canada, and the United States. These nations vied with each other to attract the professional skills which were in great demand. Jan, however, continued to scan the openings in Holland, although his hopes were dashed time and time again by the paralyzing welter of regulations and long waiting lists.

He even examined one prospect in the city of his birth, Rotterdam. It was a small townhouse close to the tunnel passing under the Maas River—a hole in the ground spewing forth vast volumes of noise and car exhaust. The musty waiting room had been stripped of everything except some crude benches. Heavy traffic passed right in front of the house, which stood in the middle of a high crime area. Obviously, this was no place to bring up children, so Jan went back to gamble with the advertisements in the medical journals.

The American medical establishment could not meet the demand for training, so many war veterans were forced to study overseas. Jan, who had met some of these veterans, was impressed by their valiant struggle to study in a foreign tongue. He began to investigate the east and west coast of America, since he needed the proximity of the ocean. Jan knew he would never feel really comfortable in the mountains or on the plains. One of his sisters had immigrated to Montreal, but the medical regulations were unusually stiff there and the climate too severe for him. He soon discovered an attractive opening in the Pacific Northwest city of Tacoma, in Washington. This state was one of the few permitting Jan to take the state board exams and practice after only one year of internship. Elsewhere, it would take two to five years.

All this indecision put a considerable strain on Maryke, now pregnant for the third time. She disliked Rotterdam intensely. She had no friends and the murky cloud of her husband's past still hovered about them. Willem, who continued to rail against his own persecutions, only intensified their discontent. The Dutch were now fiercely anti-German and preoccupied with witch-hunts and settling old scores. Jan's applications to the local hospitals meant that many people knew about his past. Of course, he would have to reveal all if he applied for an American visa and immigration approval. But Jan felt he had to take a chance, since nothing in Holland satisfied him.

In due course, Jan was asked to present himself for an interview in Paris. The train journey was an anxious one. He knew he would have to face yet another combative inquisition by the FBI and handle a barrage of pointed, prying questions. But again he triumphed. They accepted this thirty-year-old, ex-SS soldier as a potential citizen of the United States.

Jan and his family could now leave. But there was one condition set by Maryke that would be extremely difficult to fuflfill. She would immigrate to America only if her baby could be delivered at home. Jan agreed, not fully cognizant that contrary regulations prevented this in their new country.

After a long and tedious flight, they landed in New York (once known as New Amsterdam) at a time when new airport buildings were under construction and the customs and immigration offices were housed in temporary barracks. The hot and humid air greeted them like an open oven. The place was teeming with people rushing about feverishly, without human interaction. Jan was struck by the sight of high-heeled elegant black ladies surging forward with a delicate measured haste and focused intent. His little daughter nervously wondered why there were so many "Black Peters" about. She referred to the traditional December the 5th festival of Saint Nicholas celebrated in Holland. This is when Saint Nicholas arrives from Spain and rides his great white horse through the city streets while Black Peter, an aggressive little black fellow, scuttles about with cookies and gifts for the good children. Those who had behaved badly the previous year risked being thrown in Black Peter's sack and carried off to Spain.

Everything felt vividly unusual. Streams of people were arriving and leaving—so much destiny in motion. Everyone was a stranger with a hidden past, sharing but an infinitesimal glimpse of themselves in passage to a personal destination. Jan's senses were acutely sensitive to the strange smells, sounds, and the astonishing variety of physiognomies.

The airline had misplaced the reservations for Tacoma, and Jan scrambled from office to office trying to sort it all out in stumbling English while Maryke and the children waited, a pitifully huddled clump of souls and baggage camped in the eye of a storm. They were the archetypal immigrants; expectant, overwhelmed, tired, and forlorn. But Maryke hung on. Jan had signed a medical paper stating that she could fly safely, but after eight months of pregnancy there was always a very real risk. He had to certify that she was not over thirty-two weeks pregnant. Later, an official discovered that Jan had declared she was not over thirty-two months pregnant!

Jan had previously contacted some people in Tacoma, one of them being a Dutch doctor. He had inquired about the kinds of people living in the Puget Sound area. The terse and bland reply stated that there were some nice people and some that were not so nice. He had also contacted a pastor of a Lutheran church, who greeted the family at the airport before taking the bedraggled newcomers to a home in the north end of Tacoma.

That very night Maryke went into labor, obviously induced by the intense stress of the harrowing journey. What could Jan do? He had brought some equipment with him, knowing she would refuse the American hospital no matter how desperate her condition. He had gleaned a little experience in childbirth while in his internship, but was it enough? Despite the predictable stages of labor and delivery, there is always a chance of the unexpected—there is always some element of risk.

Both previous children had been born at home in Holland. Jan had assisted the family physicians and a nurse was always present. These nurses were a great blessing, appearing when labor began and staying on a week after the birth, taking care of the children, cooking the breakfast, and cleaning the house. Should complications arise, there was always an ambulance available and a hospital on alert. The Dutch system was a fairly safe one; in fact, Holland had the highest infant survival rate in the world. Maryke refused the hospital, unappreciative of the fact that in America home deliveries were considered malpractice and highly unethical. Fortunately, the cramps subsided and then ceased altogether. She still had a couple of weeks before completing her natural term, which gave them a little breathing room to make arrangements and settle into their Tacoma home.

Tacoma, in 1949, was the major center of commerce in Puget Sound. This thriving port city, this westcoast Rotterdam with its smelting plants, pulp mills, and docks along Commencement Bay, had the forests and Cascade Mountains for a glorious backdrop. Presiding over the city to the south towered the imposing presence of Mount Rainier, a snow-capped volcano over fourteen thousand feet in height, which brooded or smiled depending on the temperament of the prevailing wind. Jan was surprised by the vast stretches of water and forest, the large houses with spacious lawns around them. There was so much space and wood compared to Holland's highly concentrated apartment buildings of concrete and brick. Naturally, Jan cast an envious eye on the local marinas packed with sailboats.

Two weeks later, Maryke went into labor again, but by this time Jan had found two responsive doctors willing to minister in the little house. He had also secured the support of the local obstetrician, who agreed to stand by at the hospital should he be needed. The Tacoma Main, in fact, had done much to pioneer the successful practice of caudal anesthesia as a safe method of pain management for long and problematic labors. The negative side of these techniques tended to prolong labor, and delivery had to be performed with forceps and episiotomy. This methodology became more and more a part of the childbirth scene and teaching programs, until the mounting pressure for more natural procedures began to take effect. Jan had begun his internship in the obstetrics department, but most patients retained their own physician, so he spent a lot of time just hanging about. Consequently, he did not receive all that much experience with the new techniques of pain relief. The birth, however went exceedingly well, much to the surprise of the attending doctors; and the helpful obstetrician willingly signed the birth certificate of the tiny immigrant.

The helpful church folk assisted the family's search for a small house. Jan was highly impressed with the young pastor, a lively internationally minded fellow who later became the president of the Lutheran World Council of Churches. They found a suitable dwelling with two bedrooms, a living room, and a small kitchen. Maryke was delighted to see the lawns and flower beds, especially the ubiquitous rhododendrons relishing the climate and enhancing the arrival of the northwest spring. They could see the water through the spaces between the houses. Despite the peculiar, even notorious, odor of the pulp mills, Jan rejoiced in the pleasing harmony of land, air, and water.

Their few belongings would take a season to arrive via the Panama Canal. Jan had sadly sold his beloved symbol of freedom—his small sailboat, but he did crate his large mahogany desk made in Rotterdam. His salary of $250 a month had to cover rent, food, clothes, and the bus rides to and from the hospital. To equip his new household with the basics, he was forced to borrow money from Holland.

Jan had little opportunity to explore the area, since his internship in the emergency departments of the Tacoma Main and the local children's hospital claimed most of his hours. Communication in English was a particularly annoying barrier he struggled with in the beginning, always having to ask someone else to talk on the phone to anxious parents and families. Much of Jan's time was spent in the obstetrics ward, but since most doctors treated and delivered their own patients, real experience was hard to come by. It was better at night on emergency duty where Jan benefitted from hands-on experience while assisting in surgery. Working in the operating theater, Jan was often bitterly reminded that he was still very much a foreigner. Just then, the World Series was about to open, with all its customary hype and anticipation. How could he comprehend the words "World Series" when baseball was totally unknown to most of the world? The lively nurses and surgeons often exchanged jokes around the operating table, but Jan, despite all the concentration he could muster, would invariably miss the point. He felt quite the alien when everyone shook with laughter while he stood nursing feelings of stupidity.

Jan, one of the first interns to arrive in July, was soon joined by a young English doctor and some from the Philippines. They worked in rotation as part of a program designed by a doctor Jan grew to admire for his responsive and friendly demeanor. Always solicitous of their personal transitions and professional welfare, his barbecues and dinner parties introduced them to the habits, menus, and festivals of the uninhibited American way of life. Later on, this kindly doctor was extremely supportive when Jan opened his own practice.

In the meantime, despite his day duties and nightly emergencies, Jan studied as best he could for his state board exams. Approaching the university to borrow old exam papers, a commonplace practice in Europe, his plea was dismissed with cold disdain. He even considered attending classes, but the university insisted he fulfill the full program, which would take him several years. Jan found the new methods of testing peculiar, to say the least. The new-fangled idea of multiple-choice questions unnerved him. Fancy shoving the tip of your pencil in a tiny hole, dooming yourself to a "yes or no," "not feasible," "all," or "none"! He was comfortable with the European system of working closely with a professor, where one's written answers were detailed and as fully explanatory as possible—a process natural to autonomous minds. It seemed to Jan as if American medicine tried hard to masquerade as an exact science. He agreed that scientific method is a necessary component of medical practice, but its real essence involves intuition, imagination, and experience—more art than science.

After working all day, he returned home to a siege of scampering or crying children. The small table in the bedroom corner, piled high with weighty medical tomes, was where Jan labored into the early hours of the morning, compelled to cover all the basic subjects again, and in a new language.

Yet despite the shortage of funds, day and night work, family needs, a demanding study program, Jan felt he was gaining control of his life. The robustness of a willpower fire forged by adversity was a trustworthy servant. In later decades, it would become his master. Maryke, on the other hand, could not yet feel any such exhilaration, dominated as she was by the household and bouts of homesickness. It was virtually impossible to properly connect and deepen a relationship with a husband who lived as if fleeing from an avalanche.

After a year of prodigious effort, Jan passed his state board exams and completed his internship. It was a true triumph of directed will. Now he was poised to grasp the next increment of independence; he was ready to establish his own practice.

Abrim with optimism, Jan opened his medical office in a tiny basement directly across from the hospital, consisting of a one-room office and dingy waiting room. Despite its modest dimensions, this was an oasis of freedom where he could construct and fit the next rung to his ladder of autonomy. His office adjoined one belonging to a physiotherapist, another World War II veteran, who had fought his way up along the spine of Italy. They became staunch friends; indeed, Jan always felt drawn to those who had survived the brutal psychological damage inflicted by violent combat. Such colleagues always gave each other good counsel, this brotherhood of trauma being a dynamic ingredient in the process of human reconstruction.

Jan relished his unfettered expansion. For once, the wind was squarely at his back. He had little free time to devote to his family, but when possible he whisked them off into the glorious nature of the northwest. This first flush of success moved him to offer his assistance to friends who were graduating from the medical school in Leiden. Several responded, and the following year saw five newly qualified doctors arrive with their families to begin their internship at Tacoma Main. Jan was delighted to smooth their difficult transitions and enjoyed discussing medicine again in his mother tongue.

After a highly satisfying first year, which had revived his finances, Jan searched for a more suitable house for his growing family. This would be his first venture into the real-estate market, one which soon quickened his interest in the tricky world of speculative investment.

They chose a large house with spacious lawns and gardens. The considerable outside work needed to maintain the grounds brought much pleasure to Maryke, offering much needed relief from the demands of child-rearing, and compensated for the fleeting presence of her husband, now increasingly engaged in the welfare of more and more patients. Her social life had lagged a long way behind his, but now Maryke could find precious moments of peace by escaping into her garden and by entertaining the families of the growing Dutch community.

The touchy issue of home delivery· resurfaced. This time, however, they were blessed by the highly competent ministration of Jan's office nurse and two doctors he knew well. Maryke, indeed, was the pioneer. It would not be long before all the local Dutch families had their home births, too. The deliveries of their fourth and fifth children in the large house restored to Jan the uniquely sacred experience of presiding over a home birth. Such moments, where mother, father, and physician conjured new life through its grand transition, its entrance into mortal space and time, were undeniably a religious experience for all present. The roles of priest and doctor merged in this sacred ceremony of emergence. Jan believed that the ever-pristine awe of the birth miracle bestows on the physician an indispensable sense of proportion, dispelling any tempting arrogance contaminating the medical mentality. Yet, despite the holy mystery of birth, Jan faced, as he always would, the chastening fear of his own Damoclean judgement. The delivery process can result in fatality, deformity, or severe disability. It was an emotional dilemma that would never be dispersed by time or by experience.

As his practice matured and his life broadened, so other themes inscribed in previous years began to break through to the surface. Jan began to resurrect his interest in the design and function of architecture. This was a powerful, though raw, impulse proportionate to the force in those indelible images of mass destruction inscribed in his war memories. In this period, Jan also began to organize medical meetings. This meant having to learn the art of diplomacy; how to bring people with diverse ideas together; how to set the forum, direct, moderate, and initiate ideas and projects; how to listen and submit to the will of the group. Many of these gatherings of family physicians were held in the retreat atmosphere of the Crystal Mountain Resort, which lay about seventy-five miles southeast of Tacoma in the glorious Cascade Mountains. Such interludes offered Jan the much-needed relaxation of skiing, not to mention the companionship and respect of his peers.

All this hyperactivity of a will set at a full throttle meant that Jan was, to all intents and purposes, an absentee father. As far as the family sanctum was concerned, he was, at best, a peripheral role model. He trusted that this unavoidable lack would be balanced by his offspring awakening their own powers of self-reliance and independence—as he himself had done. Jan made every effort, however, to lead them out into the world by exploring the magnificent nature lathering the northwest mountains and coastline. Jan taught his children to ski, climb, ride, and fish. They all learned to sail, to respond instinctively to the play of changing tide and wind. He deliberately set them personal challenges away from home—away from the stultifying limitations of school and city life. As a father he wished to engender in them the faculties of self-reliance, self-control, and initiative. Jan admired their natural intelligence, but he wished to foster in them the same measure of volitional power that had carried him through his bitter defeats, squalid despair, and infantile dreads. He believed that such early experiences would inhabit and sustain their adult years. As far as Jan was concerned, there was nothing better he could bequeath them.

Of course, he clashed with the school authorities when he spontaneously whisked them away to mountain or coast to reveal the world of will and action. He had little interest in organized team sports, which to him appeared as extensions of rigid control exercised by others. No, Jan wished to promote individuality and independence. But yet, this too is but one developmental lobe in every child's psyche. He totally ignored their inner emergence—the awakening devotional, emotional, and social senses. Jan's own pathological need for liberty blinded him to the other half of a child's passage to maturity. But more, his fierce determination to resist control blocked the perception that his very insistence on liberty was, itself, a form of control he imposed on others. It was a paradox that would unwittingly endanger all his relationships, especially those with his children.

This first half of Jan's thirty-year cycle confirmed his irrepressible surge towards career accomplishments and the independence he had always yearned for. The steady growth of his medical work, organizational involvement, and good standing in the medical fraternity served to nourish Jan's self-esteem, at least in the surface elevations of his psyche. Jan's industrious temperament, his ability to laser focus his will and cut through obstacles was a perfect match for the free enterprise system—the hallmark of American opportunism.

The theme of architectural design woven into the fabric of Jan's destiny as far back as his Delft days, later reinforced by the mass destruction of European habitation, now resurfaced as a definable impulse. Jan's ancestral bloodstream stirred in his present. Some of his relatives had been ship builders, a lineage extending far back into Holland's golden age of exploration and trade. Once, Jan himself had hoped to become a naval architect, but his practical experience, the denouement of working in inclement weather and incessant noise, not to mention the abrasive conflict between management and unions, changed Jan's mind and his direction. This proved to be a fortunate decision, since the ship-building industry in Europe collapsed when the cheap labor of the Rising Sun greedily grabbed the world market.

Jan's first building project was a modest one. He redesigned his own house, adding a large carport, a bomb shelter, and a spacious studio for Maryke, who had recovered her interest in art, especially sculpture. He also converted the garage into a luxurious bedroom with a modernized bathroom. This was no mere exercise in opulence.

So many immigrants contrive ways to compensate for past privations and Jan was no exeption. He often recalled the numbing cold of his early life, the pitiful heating, and the tiny bathrooms of his native land. Folk from the spatially compressed towns of Europe could not help but be astonished, even bewitched, by the palatial American bathrooms with their fancy counters, immodest mirrors, sunken baths, and gold-plated showers. The fancy bombshelter beneath the house was a memorious concession to Jan's past. Old panics were reactivated, fanned by the almost paranoidal gesturing of the Cold War. Two entrances, one from the garden, the other inside the house, led down to a heavily reinforced chamber spacious enough for a dozen people. The tiers of bunks could be folded back against the walls. The large room contained a shower and stocks of food and water, besides an extensive array of medical supplies and equipment, not to mention a liberal supply of wine.

When thirty-six, Jan decided to tackle a much more ambitious project. His ascending financial fortunes now permitted him to consider investment as a hopeful means of translating his daily work into forms providing future security for his family. Jan was one of several doctors combining their assets to purchase a large parcel of land in Tacoma. Their interest in building a new hospital had been generated by the mutually hostile competitiveness of the two major Tacoma hospitals—Tacoma Main and Saint Michaels. Plans were drawn for an ultramodern facility functioning at a lower tempo, dedicated to more personal expressions of family care.

This hospital later proved itself to be a highly successful venture. The location was ideal and the design and construction were of the highest quality, incorporating the latest technology and engineering. The Moreland project, initiated when Jan was thirty-six, played a major role in his life for twelve years. He designed his own office, using the contemporary style of skylights and wall hangings to give his waiting room a comforting, optimistic feeling about it.

Here in Moreland, Jan's minority and welfare patients grew by leaps and bounds. Having his office within the hospital complex gave Jan convenient access to the fine array of services, and he was able to assist in surgery during his lunch times. Of course, there were numerous obstacles to test the mettle of his will. The hospital ran into serious financial trouble, which drove Jan perilously close to bankruptcy. A major reorganization was called for, and Jan, together with a small group of doctors, took over the management. His daily life became inextricably involved with the operation of the hospital. Working on finances with doctors, Jan discovered, was guaranteed to exacerbate the volume of acids in even the strongest stomach. He found his colleagues to be a caustic, imperious brood, prone to prima-donna complexes, always grumbling about high overheads and excessive taxes. Jan, however, managed the facility until it was sold, thus freeing himself to pursue other interests.

How he was exhilarated by a fresh challenge! This time Jan invested his enthusiasm, ideas, and funds in a new project—an ambitious amalgam of townhouses, apartment complexes, garden apartments and high-rises. The location was a magnificent one overlooking the Narrows, that deep and turbulent channel between Tacoma and the Peninsula through which ocean waters circulated in and out of the Sound. The design was undertaken by a Canadian architect from Vancouver, supported by Canadian engineers. These high-rise components proved to be financially impractical, but the overall result was aesthetically pleasing and technically outstanding.

Jan found himself becoming increasingly fascinated by the social significance of architecture. He and another doctor took alternate one-year terms managing the initiative. Jan gained invaluable experience by working closely with the on-site manager. But again, like the Moreland Hospital, the financial burdens became prohibitive. Fortunately, they were able to sell it in a favorable market. On the whole, Jan found real estate to be more rewarding, financially, than his medical work. Although his practice was healthy, his growing concentration on the welfare sector, with its lower rates of reimbursement, proved to be far less remunerative than his property speculation.

Through such investments Jan was able to provide his offspring with the kind of security which later supported their education and careers. During this period he added a condominium near Lake Chelan in the Cascades, and one close to the Moclips River on the Pacific Coast. Such speculations, however, were always a gamble with so many variables like mortgage rates, depreciation, and capital-gains regulations. But this was an effusive period in the American economy when apartment and commercial buildings were used to reduce personal taxes. For Jan, they were lucrative years, and his dependents received the benefits while Jan himself gathered the design experience necessary for later projects.

Jan also acquired a small sailboat in this period—a Port Madison, which he could tow behind his car. The revived excitement of sailing soon whetted his desire for a much larger vessel, one the whole family could crew. It was not a status symbol, but rather a means of reconnecting himself with his enduring love of the sea. This thirty-four footer was part of Jan's sea-freedom equation. With so many stressful demands on his life, Jan sought an escape for himself and his family.

Their first voyage took the family north among the Canadian Islands. After a prolonged struggle against the notorious currents close to Galona Island, smoke began to pour from the engine perilously close to the fuel tank. By drifting backwards for several hours, they were able to dock in Maple Bay, where they watched the first moon landing on television while the boat was being repaired.

Sailing became a regular family occupation and Jan's children quickly acquired the nautical skills needed to navigate and maneuver the large boat. His teenage son's maiden voyage, however, nearly ended in disaster when the boy found himself trapped and pummeled by a fierce northwesterly storm. Despite the loss of the dinghy, Diaz mustered sufficient skill to bring the battered boat through the narrow entrance of the Port Townsend harbor, much to the anxious admiration of his parents.

The family also derived much winter pleasure from skiing at the Crystal Mountain Resort. All his offspring learned to ski well, soon surpassing their parents by entering competitions. Maryke and Jan were drawn into various duties such as time-keeping and medical attendance. Soon they were off to other ski centers on Mount Baker, Mount Hood, Snoqualmie Pass, and in Oregon, their car jammed with the very latest equipment, including downhill and slalom skis, plus all the necessary clothing. The children insisted on owning the very best equipment available, which was enormously expensive. Jan, in fact, decided to buy some shares in a resort area so he could afford all the season tickets.

The first twelve years of this cycle, beginning at age thirty, had been a steady, exuberant expansion of Jan's independence and personal success. Then, when Jan was forty-two, the Vietnam conflict began in earnest, and Jan's history hurtled into his present to usurp and threaten everything he had achieved. As the conflict escalated, vividly chronicled on the TV screen, so Jan's psyche drew upon its abundant store of horrors past. Again, he found himself watching the barbaric slaughter of innocents caught in a conflict devoid of clear objectives and personal meaning. He saw the American mind at large disengaging itself from the numbing platitudes of politicians and generals. It was all too real.

Soon Jan began to meet veterans riddled and dismembered by shrapnel and emotional traumas, facing the same chilling misunderstandings he had suffered long ago. He feared that his own sons, perhaps even he himself, might be ensnared by the widening net of the military draft; indeed, several doctors in his own hospital had been called to duty. Jan's instincts knew what to do. Galvanized by fear, he made feverish plans to flee with his family to Canada. Calling on the support of friends and contacts in Vancouver, he also applied for a medical license. But the crisis subsided, and the black bats spewing forth from dark caves of memory returned to their resting place.

Jan made several trips to Europe in this cycle. At Delft he met several old friends who had studied architecture and engineering with him. Jan was astonished to see the routine tranquility of their settled lives, with their comfortable incomes, comfortable careers, and comfortable family circumstances. Once all the initial questions were answered, the conversation tapered off into disengaged politeness. They were strangers to him, obviously incapable of imagining Jan's American way of life, with its challenge, pace, ambition, variety, and opportunity. They had nestled into a highly regulated, undisturbed, and comparatively sedated existence. Yes, Jan still felt like an outcast in his own homeland among these square pegs perfectly set in square holes.

At forty-five, the epochal midpoint of this cycle, Maryke initiated their first visit to the Soviet Union. For years she had longed to visit the famous Hermitage in Leningrad, to see the exquisite work of the Dutch masters collected by Peter the Great. They flew to Holland, then through the Iron Curtain into Leningrad Airport. After being thoroughly searched and questioned, with particular emphasis given to the amount of cash they were carrying, Jan and Maryke took lodging in an old-fashioned hotel. The bathroom was surprisingly primitive. One faucet, optimistically marked "hot," offered little except a trickle of dubious, cold, brown liquid. Jan felt uneasy since their room in this "approved" lodge was probably bugged by the KGB. The old lady, seemingly glued permanently to her foyer chair watching all the comings and goings, was obviously the official observer. The dining room, decorated like a military mess hall, served cold boiled eggs, tasty bread, sauerkraut, and sausages. Leaving the hotel required the approval from the Intourist office run by the KGB. Taxis were always a problem despite the lure of the almighty dollar. Their visit to the Leningrad ballet was a disaster—albeit a hilarious one. They could barely stifle their laughter when a ludicrous, stiff-jointed figure shuffled about the stage—not to mention the giant swans clumsily hauling large cartons all over the place. Returning home by the remarkably beautiful underground system suggested that all the beauty inherent in the Russian soul had been thrust down into subterranean regions. To them it seemed a perfect metaphor.

Maryke and Jan especially hoped to meet some of the people of Leningrad. After searching among the local restaurants, they were enthusiastically invited to the apartment of some students. Extremely lucky to find a taxi willing to take them, they were told, "Can't go there! Can't go there!" They slipped him what must have been a fabulous sum, but even then he dropped them off a considerable distance from their destination. The fear of being seen associating with foreigners was neurotically evident everywhere they went. Walking the gray streets among endless housing complexes identical in their mournful design and numbing grayness, Jan and Maryke passed young women wearing their sex appeal like old gray shawls. The murky corridors in the complex smelt of stale urine. The elevator was as dead as a doornail, so they climbed the poorly lit stairs before being warmly welcomed into a small apartment packed with old, middle-aged, and young people, compressed into a small box bereft of privacy. Maryke and Jan enjoyed the convivial meal, attempting to answer a barrage of questions about life in America. Trying to use the phone to call a taxi was an exercise in futility. On the street they hailed several cars, but as soon as their foreign origin was identified, the drivers sped off without them.

After much fretting, Jan and Maryke managed to find a driver willing to take them, providing they paid in dollars. Their rescuer, however, drove them all over the city, across railroad tracks, among warehouses and side streets in his effort to shake off the invisible KGB. The paranoia was staggering. Even then, he refused to take them to the hotel, which was closed when they arrived on foot. Jan tried to scale the ivy but fell. Forced to disturb the late night peace by banging on windows, they were reluctantly let in, followed by suspicious eyes. The following day they left for the airport, where again they were searched and questioned: "How much did you spend? Where are your receipts?" One official discovered that Jan had two passports—one current and one obsolete. Jan was vehemently accused of profiteering this highly prized form of currency and then taken to a room to be stripped and interrogated. Jan had visions of being carted off to Siberia, but they let him go.

Their arrival in Copenhagen prompted a celebration. Jan bought Maryke a necklace, and they relished the colorful well-stocked shops, the lively, well-dressed shoppers, the brightly lit freedom. The trip had been a tense and harrowing experience, but Maryke was well satisfied with the glorious old masters in Hermitage. With the exception of the art, the underground, and a few personal contacts, Leningrad displayed every sign of the stark morbidity of the repressed Russian spirit.

Back in Tacoma, Jan's medical work was, by now, well established in his elegant, self-designed offices in Moreland. Like his father four decades previously, Jan was increasingly involved in the service of minorities and welfare cases. In the second half of this cycle he also felt more disposed to some of the fresh initiatives proffered by the holistic concepts of healing. Although still very much a traditionalist, the old rebel examined with interest some of the new advances emerging at the periphery of orthodox medicine. Attracted by the idea of a more integrated variety of treatments, viewing the patient from a psychological as well as physiological point of view, Jan realized that institutionalized medicine, with its prevalent mechanistic-biochemical image of the ailing body and mind, could never provide all the answers. He believed that much of the conservative medical outlook was encumbered by its preoccupation with disease rather than the broader vision of true health.

From time to time Jan had reimmersed himself in the stressful study required for recertification. He took his board certification in New York when he was forty-three, his family practice at forty-nine, and another in Portland when he was fifty-six.

During this period Jan's work became more and more entangled in the sticky legal webs of medicine as his caseload of personal injuries grew, particularly neck and back traumas. This drew him into a distracting confrontation with his old archenemy—authority. Indeed, towards the close of this cycle, the saturnine theme of conflict and encounter began to reassemble its demons, then assert its distressing presence on Jan's peace of mind.

When he was fifty-four, Jan was accused of fraud by the Welfare Department. This legal joust was essentially a matter of incorrect coding with respect to the type of physical examinations given. A new system of paperwork had recently been installed, and Jan's enormous caseload of almost ten thousand patients a year ran afoul of it. Very few physicians took on welfare work because of its poor remuneration, not to mention the cumbersome weight of paperwork and the intruding nose of bureaucratic supervision. Things looked bad for a while, and Jan was forced to engage his own attorney. The outcome of all this haggling resulted in Jan's reimbursing the state $50,000. No matter how he felt about his welfare clientele, he began to reduce its size, posthaste.

At fifty-nine, just at the time conflict and disruption erupted in full force throughout every sector of his life, Jan was slammed with a malpractice suit from a patient who had taken too many tranquilizers over a long period. Jan was accused, together with the Swiss manufacturer, of negligent supervision. The patient had developed dyskinesia tarde from a medication being used extensively throughout the world. The high doses applied in mental institutions occasionally produced tremors similar to those of Parkinson's disease. Apparently the patient had continued using the prescription, and the pharmacy, under new management, had failed to notify his office. The suit was settled out of court by both the manufacturer and Jan. Facing the inquisitional maneuvers of cantankerous legal brains, Jan found, was not all that different to his dispiriting experiences with the SS and the FBI.

A year later he was forced to confront an infinitely more dangerous investigation by the Ethics Committee, which accused him of referring too many patients to physiotherapists, biofeedback experts, counselors, and rehabilitation people. This pitiless, at times ruthless, inquiry caused Jan acute stress at a time when the very fabric of his life was unraveling. This time Jan had to suffer the withering denunciation and suspicion of his peers without legal representation. It was essentially a clash of philosophies—with strong monetary overtones. Jan had worked intently to reduce his patients' dependence on medication by organizing a broader, more holistic schedule, involving a team of physiotherapists, counselors, and vocational rehabilitation people. He wanted his injured patients to adjust to their traumas and bring their lives back to productivity and balance. This meant counseling and involvement with the powerful emotive forces in healing responsible for restoring self-confidence.

Despite heartening successes, Jan found himself being critically scrutinized by his peers, facing a very real threat to his license and livelihood. Of course, the Ethics Committee was justified in monitoring medical integrity, protecting the rights of the patient in the face of the mounting quackery at large. But Jan also met the stagnant minds of orthodoxy, minds suffering from the medical myopia born from fears of alternative methodology. He faced the old guard whose visionary arteries were clogged by the sclerotic sediments of conservatism. Jan felt that nowhere in medicine was there a greater need for courageous imagination than in the burgeoning complexities of medical ethics. The committee withdrew its charges, fully accepting Jan's explanation of his treatments. Naturally, with his past, this agonizing inquisition opened old wounds. Once again Jan was being told what he could do and what he could not do. All the tension of this episode contributed to the total collapse of his equilibrium.

Earlier, Jan's forty-ninth year had opened a seven-year phase dominated by the deteriorating cohesion of his family. As the internal strains grew, so the fragile crust of family solidity was rent by numerous fissures, caused primarily by the remorseless decay of his marriage. At this point it took little to convert hair-line cracks into unbridgeable chasms.

Conflicts over money loaned for educational purposes brought all the suspicion and distrust to boil. The family conference called to solve the situation quickly degenerated into a full-blown uproar. Maryke sided with her son and everyone chose sides, thus shattering the semblance of family unity. It would never recover.

All this dissention was undoubtedly fueled by the morbid condition of Jan's marriage. All too often, home was rife with bitter recriminations and the querulous bitching of downright hostility, painfully demonstrating to everyone just how far Maryke and Jan had grown apart. This was not really surprising. For years Jan had channeled all his energy into his career and special projects. Domestic nurturing and emotional support had fallen by the wayside years before. The crystallizing roles of housewife and career-smith were typical of most of the doctors who had brought their families from Holland, and divorce seemed to be the inevitable handmaiden of neglect. Maryke had given up years ago. She had loved her husband deeply but realized Jan could never nourish, or even acknowledge, her emotional needs. Of course, he had provided for her physical welfare, but his attitude was matter-of-fact, dutybound, and pragmatic; there were no heart connections. Their family life had been shaped by external forces—little nourished its heart. Marriage, that miraculous process of mutual transformation, could never survive this emotional neglect.

Jan's psychological constitution found it wellnigh impossible to allow anyone close to the ultrasensitive zones of his vulnerability, those regions of his psyche storing the hurts and abuses of his past, all milling round the throne of his self-esteem. He spent less and less time at home and began a string of indiscreet love affairs, all of which followed the same pattern. They would open with a flare of attraction followed by a rapid ripening, only to conclude with withdrawal, disengagement, and, more often than not, petulance. His barriers were too impenetrable. The length of the affair depended on how determined the lady was to scale Jan's impossibly high ramparts. The closer Jan grew towards these women, the more discomfort he felt. He would inevitably interpret this as being caused by his lover's efforts to control him; indeed, Jan had hair-trigger reflexes in this area.

In many respects, Jan remained an enigma to his women. They found him charming, energetic, and sensual, stimulated by variety and challenge, to all intents and purposes the epitome of the successful male. Few of them saw his defensive sense of self blocking his sense of the other.

Jan's family disputes rocked his foundations, ill-equipped as he was to manage anger and recrimination, which had a direct conduit into his past. So he escaped to seek warmth in the soporific glow of yet another love affair. How he yearned for warmth, yet he was powerless to sustain it. The first flush of eros and amour was inevitably followed by the repulsion generated by the engine of Jan's fear. His women could never accept nor understand it.

Jan's life was a triumph of will supported by natural intelligence. The vultures tearing his happiness to shreds lived in his emotional desert. He invariably looked outwards for the solution to his woes—not bearing to peer into his interior and face the old demons ruling there. This, however, was the only real sanctum of his salvation—and this was his tragedy.

Jan completely lost his footing in his mid fifties, expending more and more energy on his wild dance of distraction. Yet his partying, heavy drinking, and lady chasing were nothing more than a vain attempt to find something that could be discovered inside himself. All this worried his friends and scandalized his family, wreaking havoc on both his personal and professional associations.

The divorce agreement, signed when he was fifty-six, after thirty years of marriage, was a complex legal arrangement covering much more than Maryke's security. By now Jan had sufficient assets to establish a trust fund, providing a comfortable financial umbrella for the rest of Maryke's life.

Despite the irrevocable death process within her marriage, Maryke, in her faithfulness, felt bitterly betrayed by her husband's almost pathological interest in other women; she could never forgive his deceptions. For good or ill, their destinies had been joined for three decades. Despite the numerous episodes of turmoil and now the finality of her change of status, Maryke felt the rightness of her release. She knew she had loved her husband well.

Perhaps she would always love him on one eternal level of destiny. No matter how maddening he could be, she knew Jan could only do what he had done. He had made his choices, but they were compulsive solutions, never free decisions.

For years Maryke had known that their fettered wedlock was dependent on her submissiveness, and this the spirit of her heart could never accept. They could never solve their differences because Jan viewed every kind of conflict as a form of war. He considered all argument to be a personal rejection. Thus, their squabbles were inflammations of dominance, control, and power. Maryke would never accept dominance of any kind, but this was all Jan could accept. Maryke was a sculptor. She desired a three-dimensional rapport, of depth, breadth, and volume, room for her personality to breathe and grow. She saw Jan was condemned to live on one of appearance rather than depth and substance. She dared not rise or fall into the other dimension of tolerant gray space necessary for healthy communication, but Jan saw everything in terms of black and white. It was too painful for Maryke.

Thus Jan was powerless to redeem those old patterns which gripped him so strongly. He was clamped in the vise of his past, unable to welcome the redemptive, healing opportunity of the present and future. All Maryke wanted to do now was to breathe and expand into the unthreatened space of her art and garden. While Maryke retired to her garden, her poetry and sculpture, Jan fled from all the bickering and hostility. Somehow he had to build his dikes higher and higher to protect himself from the rising waters of despair. He visited Sun Valley, Orlando, and Spain, soaking up the hyperactivity, entertainment, and attentive women. He desperately needed to be accepted. Suspecting that others could not understand him, Jan hoped, at least, that they would treat him well and show him the respect he missed at home.

While attending a medical meeting a few weeks after the divorce, a friend suggested his obviously dispirited colleague apply for the position of ship's doctor on a cruise liner touring the Hawaiian Islands. Jan jumped at the idea. This would be an idyllic escape on a thirty-thousand-ton love boat, complete with salary, free meals, two swimming pools, luxurious dining rooms, and time-off ashore. Here were all the enchantments needed to restore Jan's spirit and bury his recent traumas under new sensations.

The higher the expectation, the worse the denouement. Jan's tiny cabin stood on the waterline next to the cramped, medieval hospital room, a chlythonic grotto of vibration. His senses were bombarded with the whine of obsolete air-conditioners, generators, pumps, rudder mechanisms—a broad range of frequencies and amplitudes guaranteed to melt his neural systems. How on earth was it possible to check heart sounds and blood pressures? The ship, moreover, had been reactivated after fifteen years of dormancy; there were leaks everywhere. In fact, just before Jan boarded, sewage had swilled through his deck. Jan's nose confirmed the fact that the hasty clean-up left much to be desired.

Jan's new hospital had to serve eight hundred passengers. Making cabin visits was a perilous affair, scrambling up ladders and stairs with pockets stuffed with pills and syringes. Even more harrowing were the acrobatic maneuvers required to carry a patient down to Jan's subterranean chamber. Stitching lacerations had to be an eürythmic exercise performed in concert with the roll of the ship. Instead of palm trees, wine, and romance, Jan found himself beleaguered by helpless drunks or the shameless clutchings of persistent homosexuals. He wondered why he always ended up feeling trapped. His frustration, however, soon reached the level needed to escape. Managing to slip past the guards, he took a taxi to the airport and flew home, leaving the ship stranded in port for several days until another gullible doctor could be requisitioned.

As if to further emphasize the past re-entering the present, Jan's parents arrived in Tacoma. Cornelia and Willem had moved from their house in Spain to the dry warmth of Arizona, hoping to soothe Cornelia's arthritic condition. Jan invited them to Tacoma to visit their grandchildren before it was too late. Cornelia suffered from rheumatism and stomach ailments, which required surgery, but Willem was remarkably active for his years, despite recent surgery for prostate problems. Jan moved out of his apartment to his sailboat, and his parents moved in.

The euphoria of family reunion quickly faded when familiarity awoke the old demons and their querulous antics. Cornelia's physical condition required much medical supervision. Soon after their arrival, Willem had an operation at Moreland to again relieve his prostate constrictions. This was a fine opportunity for their doctor son to be of service. Jan was, as ever, very tentative with them on a conversational level, but at least they could rely on his medical and financial protection. Indeed, they made it quite clear they fully expected their son to take care of them for the rest of their days.

This assumption set Jan a problem of some magnitude. He was acutely aware of the crippling expenses of medical treatment after knowing many patients crushed by the financial legacy of extended hospital care. Many of them lost all their assets, including their homes. Since it was obvious that both parents were prime candidates for extensive and imminent treatment, Jan searched for a solution by contacting Lloyds of London and several American insurance firms. Ineligible for Medicare, his parents would be totally exposed until a suitable coverage could be found. Jan devised a temporary solution, proposing his parents return, for a month or two, to the protective umbrella of Holland's socialized medicine, while he devised a suitable coverage for them in the United States. They could decide then to stay in Europe or return to America. His sister, Machteld, through unwell, agreed to care for them, and Jan covered the travel expenses.

Fully aware of his parents' tottering health, Jan feared to expose his own family to the catastrophic results of prolonged medical attention. To him, this seemed a reasonable proposition, but his suggestions were met by an explosion of vitriolic anger. Cornelia screamed at him, declaring that she would never leave America. Willem blasted him for being cold hearted, insisting that this ridiculous idea flagrantly demonstrated his son's hatred for them. In fact, the embittered and disgusted old man hurriedly repacked their belongings and moved to a motel. He could not bear to set eyes on his traitorous and miserly son. As usual, Jan was abysmally baffled; the more he tried to help, the worse things became.

A few days later, Jan received a terse call from a local hospital stating that his mother had died from heart arhythmia. The stress had been too much for her frailty. Feeling helpless and numbed by the terrible finality of his mother's departure across the great divide, Jan was glad he could at least bury some of his wretched guilt feelings by immersing himself in the funeral arrangements. His children managed to find a temporary apartment for Willem while Jan concentrated on the funeral details. In the meantime his brother, now a scientist in New Mexico, joined them, adding his own angers to the family stew.

Jan's eldest daughter Saskia, compassionate and caring by nature, devoted herself to supporting her distraught grandfather during and after the funeral. She, more than anyone else in the family, was intrigued by this erratically brilliant and enigmatic ancestor. Her father's obvious disdain for him did nothing to lessen Saskia's interest in learning more about her heritage. Jan, too, felt a special closeness to Saskia, but the unending family travail smothered any real chance of a rapport; indeed, not much closeness could survive the familial warfare.

After the funeral, while Cornelia's belongings were being collected, conflict flared yet again when Jan's brother sharply accused Saskia of stealing a valuable piece of Cornelia's jewelry. He also charged her with manipulating Willem's finances, even going so far as to call in the police and engage an attorney. The incendiary family forums soon dissolved into vicious attacks and counterattacks. Both Jan's father and his brother unequivocally condemned him for killing his own mother. This toxic brew of grief, guilt, and ancient resentments from the family vine contaminated everyone. Saskia's heart was shattered, and the ghastly experience left her with many scars.

Then there were the legal entanglements of Cornelia's will, which had been drawn up in Spain. The problem was truly an international one. How did Spanish law pertain to a Dutch citizen dying in the United States? The family infighting continued to the grave. For years to come there would be bickering over the family plot. Who owned what? Who paid for what?

Willem and Cornelia's marriage, spanning sixty tempestuous years, was a monumental achievement considering the imbalances in their psychological constitutions, not to mention the intolerable strain of their war years. Their partnership was dominated by a rhythm of attraction and repulsion, dependence and independence, similar to the cycles wrecking Jan's relationships. In fact, they married each other four times. In all probability the pattern would have perpetuated itself but for a weary judge who viewed this peculiar oscillation as being simply ridiculous, thus dismissing their fifth petition.

Perhaps we might expect the accruing wisdom of advancing age to encourage the powers of tolerance and forgiveness. But in their case, it seemed as if the physical process of hardening had intruded into their psychological nature. So many hoary antagonisms passed with them into the grave. Indeed, the ancestral challenge facing several generations of this family was the insoluble problem of forgiveness. This was as firmly embedded in their history as their genetic structure. Break-up and separation were seldom overcome by the forces of love, cohesion, and reconcilation. There was so much compulsion and so little freedom, despite the wealth of intelligence liberally bestowed on them all.

Immediately following this episode, another element of Jan's history reappeared to further darken the night of his present. His beloved Machteld lay critically ill with cancer. Despite her operation, chemotherapy, and considerable holistic efforts, she continued to suffer relentless pain. Jan was shocked by her appearance. Despite a life given to healing, he felt absolutely useless. She had cared for him through all of the vicissitudes of childhood and youth. She had shared his terrors and rare moments of childhood happiness. Easy-going, practical, unruffled, and soothing in emergencies, Machteld always appeared to be happy. She was the blessed peacemaker whom everyone confided in. Not that her life was spared tragedy. Her marriage to a dentist had failed miserably, and she had lost one of her two sons to rheumatoid arthritis.

Machteld's suffering became so intolerable that she seriously contemplated suicide. She discussed it with Willem, who had returned to Holland, only to have biblical admonitions hurled at her like javelins. Despite the guilt she felt for opposing her mortified father, Machteld decided to choose liberation. Jan supported her decision—to the further chagrin of his father. Euthanasia was illegal in Holland, but the political, legal, and medical tolerance was unusually strong and widespread. Machteld's fatal injection was given by a doctor in a Rotterdam clinic, also attended by an official from the Health Department, as required by law. Jan felt the loss deeply, but he was relieved to see Machteld freed from her rack of anguish. If Jan was action, Machteld was being. She alone in his family had the tenderness to comfort and bless, and he felt he had lost the better part of himself.

Despite all the loss and conflict festooning the closing years of Jan's second thirty-year cycle, totally unexpected germs of hope, fresh creative impulses, were being released for the approaching one. Two years earlier Jan had met Renee while playing tennis. It did not take him long to be attracted to this forty-five-year-old French teacher, recovering from her own release after a vigorless and atrophied marriage. There was something about Renee's eyes that touched Jan's heart.

Both were highly vulnerable, and both were starved of warmth. Jan was drawn to Renee's maturity, composure, and spirited competitiveness. Besides her natural athletic interests, Renee was a lover of French culture and fine literature. Renee also stood up well to Jan's father—he admired that. A connoisseur of fine food, Jan was naturally delighted to sample Renee's superb cooking. Renee, on her part, soon warmed to Jan's exuberant spirits, his generosity, and especially the unpretentious and undivided attention she longed for. Their relationship ripened swiftly and they decided to live together. So, despite all his turmoil, Jan had found his solace, a haven of warmth in the midst of his arctic season of discontent. But more, close to the time he lost both his sister and mother, just when the frown of death and guilt brooded over everything, Jan was absolutely staggered to discover he would become a sixty-year-old father. Right in the vortex of his crisis, the future affirmed his hope—the promise of a new beginning, another chance for renewal and the happiness he craved. It was his miracle, and he was beside himself with joyful anticipation.

* * *

I am Chronos, the meter within the stanzas of your time! Mark well the irrepressible themes of Jan's destiny—each entering and reentering at the appointed rhythmic time.

Mark well that Jan, like all others, is also embedded in the cyclic matrix of nation and universe, driven by his evolution as is the rise and fall of mammoths, empires, and solar systems. So everything becomes and passes, to become again. Your legends proclaim it. "You shall pass from the garden, through the forest, to enter the sacred city." Your religions proclaim it. "You shall pass from birth through temptation to your crucifixion and resurrection."

My task now is to disclose to you the organic reality of your timelife. Learn well from the humble plant, since it perfectly epitomizes the dynamics of the cycle. See how it replicates its form through the rhythms of the seasons. Likewise, do you journey through your seasons, the indivisible nucleus of your being ever adding to its substance and content. As every plant demonstrates a matchless image of the cycle, so does each human life.

In the beginning was the seed—the highly compressed essence, the imprinted logos of form and function—the essence of previous seasons. So it is with you: every new cycle retains, as seeds, the experience won in the preceding span. There follows the compelling drive for new growth, which is nothing less than the lengthening stem of your expansion. Thus do leaves of your actions unfurl into the world as a further exhalation of your purpose. The midpoint, the fifteenth-year fulcrum, marks the change of emphasis. Here begins a phase of inhalation as you inhale into your core your recent experiences. Now the irrepressible dynamic turns inward as the cycle moves closer to its completion. The fruit embodies this crucial interiorization—the harvest. These hidden seeds now become new impulses of will. The cycle closes, the fruit falls, cracks, explodes, decays. In this crisis, the precious germs of future change are thus released—and a new cycle is born. And so I shall lead you into Jan's closing season, tracing his themes to their conclusion. I shall indicate their movement from personal to transpersonal levels, for he, like you, is a cell in the world body, traversing its own rhythms of becoming. Jan's personal odyssey is nothing less than the spiritual transformation of the base metals of experience into the true gold of intrinsic being. This is the true alchemy of time.

Pity not our sleepwalker blundering his way through time. Judging the rightness or wrongness of his choices is as useful as being a fish with hydrophobia. Jan's anchor of confidence may drag in his storms; he may slide into temptation; his path may be littered with misjudgments; fear invades his deepest chambers. The wounded are left in his wake and Jan appears to tear down that which he has built. But he lives on, firmly set on his course.

So dwell not on spreading wrinkles, fading appetites, and hoary failures. Jan has his victories. Despite myopic blunderings and compulsions born of fear, despite the sins politicians, generals, and bureaucrats have committed in his name, despite the blind cruelties of your demoralized planet and the pains inflicted, *the universe is not disinterested*. Jan still retains his time—his quest remains. Not a fragment is misplaced, not a petal faded. He has endured, and the rhythms of his time will thrust him onward. And so it is.

Chapter IV
Constriction and Release

As Jan reached his sixtieth birthday, so he felt his infernal past release him from his shackles. From this platform of time Jan's history looked to him like a nasty, congealed lump of constriction. How relieved he was to feel its weight disperse and be replaced by youthful moods of soaring anticipation. The approaching birth of his child infused Jan's flagging will with a burst of unbridled energy, as the dense nimbus of his gloom dissolved in the magical warmth of Renee's love. Their mutual joy also touched their friends, now relieved to see their worrisome Lothario recover his equilibrium at last. Jan's miraculous stroke of fortune reminded him that Fortuna still invested herself in him. No matter what the previous disasters, life retained its confidence in him, although Jan wondered if the silver purity of these precious moments would last.

Jan's close friends surprised him by arranging a "roasting" to celebrate his sixtieth birthday. They all duly assembled at a classy country club in Tacoma for a well-lubricated banquet. Following the sumptuous meal, each of them publicly addressed Jan for his own edification. Thus, Jan had to listen to a hilarious litany of every weakness, fault, error, excess, imbalance, and paradox they had detected in him. Without mercy, Jan's friends surgically dissected every historic tissue of his aberrant behavior. Much of the humor was liberally ladled with raucous sexual comments and poems alluding to the expected loss of his infamous sexual potency. Jan could bear it. He even relished being the center of this kind of storm since the "roasting" was an expression of affection, saturated with humor. Jan could accept almost anything if applied with a strong dose of merriment, which rendered it powerless to broach his zones of sensitivity. How he revelled in the attention. There he sat, his face flushed with wine, laughter, and pride, tears in his eyes and glass in hand.

If Hippocrates, the Greek father of medicine, had been present, he would have easily identified Jan's character type by recognizing the dominant humor, as the Greeks called it, meaning the physiological energy system responsible for Jan's temperament. Jan fitted the "choleric" type to a tee, with his stocky build, short neck, dark eyes, powerful bulllike chest, strong circulation, body warmth, and especially his determined tread. Jan's personality profile also closely matched the Greek archetype. Cholerics are predominately goal-centered people, who direct their egoic force outwards into action. Being natural leaders, they have an abundance of constructive and destructive energy. Temperament, however, is a two-edged sword; this will-dominated soul of the choleric is prone to tyranny and rigidity, and the challenge of their own angers and impatience. Strong in central vision but weak in peripheral perception, such personalities are preoccupied with mastering the external world, not the interior one. Strong in their awareness of the I, they are weak in perceiving the thou. Napoleon was a prime example of this type, and Jan resembled him in many ways.

Jan and Renee's daughter was born on the winter solstice. Jan was sixty years old. He watched the auspicious sunrise that delightful day, even videotaping its auspicious splendor. Sol climbed into its day from behind Mount Rainier, which for the occasion had considerably divested itself of its customary mantle of cloud. The sky was clear, and an orange glow lit the angled snow slopes and glaciers. Jan saw it as a good omen, since the northwest Indians believed that only on this day, with the sun visibly rising from behind the volcano, can souls depart for their heavenly sojourn. Only this signal released the dead from their mortal enchantment.

The birth in Tacoma Main went surprisingly well, considering it was Renee's first child. Jan could scarcely believe it was all real. This time he would devote all his attention to his daughter, Esperanza. Yes, he would reveal the wonders of the world to her and shower all his love and life learning on her. She symbolized his hope, his phoenix rising from the ashes of travail and folly. She was his synthesis of princess, mistress, wife, and mother. Yes, Esperanza personalized the eternal feminine for Jan and her birth was for him a mystical experience.

The tempo of Jan's life accelerated as his new exuberance of will coursed through the old channels of his life's themes. Paging through an architectural journal, Jan was intrigued by the announcement of a Seattle design competition open to anyone interested in inner-city housing. Like many American cities, Seattle's inner-city area was a towering shrine to commerce—humming by day, relatively deserted at night after its commuter streams poured back across bridges and freeways to the suburbs. The burgeoning number of homeless and disadvantaged folk, not to mention the mounting traffic congestion, gave rise to much concern. This competition was devised to stimulate new thinking about housing complexes positioned between Seattle's waterfront and the high-rise apartments on higher ground.

Jan had visited Rotterdam on several occasions where he could observe the city planners and a crop of brilliant architects wrestle with the immense problems of post-war rebuilding. Like his father before him, Jan felt emotionally connected to the underprivileged, the drug addicts, the prostitutes, the homeless, the working class, and especially the growing numbers of working, yet homeless people.

Drawing on the inspiration of Rotterdam, Jan developed a proposal complete with explanatory charts and models. He was guided by an architect friend and his son, Theo, who had recently studied with one of Rotterdam's leading architects. He was delighted to work with his son, despite Theo's persistent and edgy hostility.

Jan's scheme was designed to serve the problematical mix of ethnic groups which congregate in the inner cities. His social impulse was primarily concerned with support, care, education, and self-improvement. The bottom floor, which was open, contained green areas and recreational facilities, while the second floor concentrated on services, shops, theaters, and clinics, counseling and educational facilities. Jan's plan placed strong emphasis on the personal care and healing resources of this community. It offered services for drug addicts and AIDS sufferers and included daycare centers for both the young and aged. He called it his 4-F plan. "Freedom" meant freedom from noise, pollution, crime, and loneliness. "Fellowship" involved the facilities and organizations needed to stimulate mutual enjoyment of dance, theater, and the arts. "Fairness" suggested the design of living areas where the various ethnic groups shared their unique virtues. He added a necessary fourth F, which was "Fun"—facilities for relaxation and enjoyment.

Jan took paternity leave from his medical practice to take care of his daughter and work on his design project. His desk, ten floors above ground level, overlooked the port of Tacoma. Father and daughter became a familiar sight in the early morning when Dad jogged along the waterfront paths pushing Esperanza in a large, red "baby jogger," a tricycle with enormous wheels. From time to time he would stop to introduce his little one to the local cats, dogs, and zoo creatures, while Esperanza made her first wide-eyed and wonder-filled appraisal of the world. Occasionally Jan would proudly introduce his daughter to his patients, who were walking their way to recovery after by-pass surgery.

Jan submitted his design, but the adjudicators chose a project with aesthetic attractibility but little or no social significance. They preferred form over function. The experience, however, would be of inestimable value to Jan later on.

Jan ardently pursued another new venture at this time, between age sixty and sixty-three—soccer. He had played the game as an eleven-year-old in Leyden, and later took his own children to see the Seattle Sounders, until the club went bankrupt. His own city, Tacoma, had recently experimented with a franchise from the indoor soccer league. Despite the encouraging response, the Tacoma club soon found itself in serious financial trouble. Fortunately, a group of local businessmen organized a rescue attempt and took over the franchises, and Jan decided to contribute his financial support. His primary interest, however, was a social one, since Jan believed the young professionals would be suitable role models capable of inspiring the local youth by visiting hospitals, youth clubs, drug centers, and a wide range of social events. He was also interested in finding ways to provide helpful financial and career counseling for the players themselves, since their precarious soccer careers were relatively short-lived.

It was obvious to everyone that Jan enjoyed watching his team play. He could be found at every home game, sitting behind the east-side goal or striding about greeting friends, or chasing his toddling princess all over the place. It was this involvement in soccer, however, that proved to be the vehicle of synchronicity responsible for lifting Jan's destiny from a personal onto a global platform of action.

The celebration following a game with a Moscow team drew the necessary elements together which generated the idea of an exchange of Soviet and American physicians—a vision energizing the rest of Jan's life. After the reception, he met both the Soviet and the American representatives of the Goodwill Games organization engaged in preparing the 1990 events to be held in the Seattle-Tacoma area. This convergence brought all the theme threads in Jan's past together to lift his destiny from a personal to a transpersonal level. Jan enthusiastically explored the complex ramifications of an East-West exchange program connected, for an initial boost, to the fast-approaching Goodwill Games.

Tackling the daunting array of problems with his customary zeal, Jan had to elbow his way past all the buffers and duffers of layered bureaucracy. He spent his days meeting doctors and organizations, his nights trying to communicate via the erratic Soviet telephone system. Somehow the financial and transport problems, not to mention the host program and conference itinerary, had to be solved in time for the games. Jan had to pick his way through a mine-field of obstacles and opposition, and at times it looked as if he would fail to get his divided doctor-ducks in a row in time.

While Jan's will functioned remarkably well on one level, his emotional constitution suddenly imploded into ferment and torment on another. The classical Greeks considered sixty-three to be the age most dangerous to health. For Jan it was a major psychological crisis. Although the genesis of his future was optimistically shaping his present, his past returned with hellish vengeance to thrust him into a major breakdown. He was frequently jolted by a barrage of particularly vivid and disruptive flashbacks, and again he felt he was losing control of his life. One moment he was rushing his three year old to ballet, circus, and soccer games, the next he was stuck for hours in development meetings or stricken by the attacks of his avenging demons.

Esperanza's birth drastically altered Jan and Renee's relationship. Whatever the source, his old emotional dragons re-exerted their influence until both felt threatened by the other. Jan instinctively reared away from what he assumed were Renee's attempts to control him, and he berated her for failing to support his projects. Her preoccupation with mothering left Jan feeling badly neglected.

Renee, on her part, was dismayed by Jan's all too evident withdrawal. She accused him of using Esperanza to escape, and she felt particularly bewildered by his refusal to communicate. Thus, both of them had slithered into the slough of postpartum depression following the heady exuberance of Esperanza's birth. Not only was Renee an only child herself, she had no experience whatsoever of motherhood. Jan, on the other hand, was highly experienced, and Renee valued his competent handling of baby affairs.

This should have brought them closer, but in fact the reverse happened. As tensions rose and the terror of Jan's flashbacks increased, both felt the tragic drift towards separation, but both were powerless to stop it. Despite the stress, the pace actually accelerated as Jan insisted on more and more dinner parties and trips. Renee could not understand why her partner lavished so much energy and money on costly celebrations like the baptism reception for 300 guests, or the hosting of guests from Moscow and Vladivostok, his investment in the Tacoma Stars, and the design competition. There was simply no family order, no rhythm, no balance—only hyperactivity.

Renee felt humiliated, isolated, and devastated by Jan's lack of emotional support. She had given up her teaching and was now totally dependent on Jan for everything. She felt lost and lonely as the black drapes of depression began to enfold her, when Jan, without warning, moved to his other condominium after his first reaction to his flashbacks.

The conflict between them swirled around a bewildered Esperanza, as they discovered they had opposite views on parenting. Jan abhorred what he considered Renee's rigid control and overbearing authority, based on the rule of the "no." Renee, in turn, could not accept Jan's rule of "yes," and his reckless disregard for protection by throwing his daughter into a whirligig of sense stimulation. She was convinced the child was being treated as an adult, even a mistress, used for Jan's own self-aggrandizement.

Here he was again, everything turning against him, everything turning sour. Struggling with the physicians' exchange, his relationship a vortex of emotion, Jan was also daily assaulted by flashbacks, doused by depression, and numbed by alcohol. As the schism between Jan and Renee widened, so they increasingly failed to set basic ground rules as far as Esperanza was concerned. The three year old was caught in the cross-fire; her mother wanted protection, her father exposure. No wonder the child showed signs of stress and began to play one off against the other. As their relationship moved inextricably towards litigation, Jan set up a trust fund for his daughter and gave Renee a liberal allowance. But what about the future? What about the custody question?

The Goodwill Games opened while Jan stood in the eye of his hurricane, offering him desperately needed comradeship, hope, and distraction. While the seams of his psyche were being split open, Jan's successes were clear to see. Jan's temperament, however, seldom acknowledged his own victories since his long view of life invariably locked on to his seductive visions of the future. Jan's real achievements, the true completions, were never given proper acceptance. He never stood still long enough.

Seattle and Tacoma in the summer of 1990 displayed the genuine exuberance and anticipation of hosting the games. There were countless welcoming celebrations, exhibitions, and conferences—cultural reciprocity at every level. The prickly nationalism completely usurping the Olympic ideals of the Greeks was missing here. People celebrated people, meeting as human beings, not ideologues or political or military pedants. The absence of fear, despite the intense security arrangements, was emblematic of this altogether remarkable year of change.

The Soviet folk soul had chosen President Gorbachev as its John the Baptist. He, according the personal rhythms of his own destiny, had intersected the greater cycles of world destiny. In the right place at the appointed time, Gorbachev was the Turner of the Key, his task being to twist the ponderous key of the Kremlin identity and thrust the door open a crack. The winds of the age would do the rest and bring fresh air into a land asphyxiated by its own staleness. The shift in the global mind in the past year had astounded even the aristocrats of pessimism, leaving in its rear legions of postmortem experts and think tanks swallowing their own intellectual dust. The world had moved. Something had shifted, like the piece of apple in Snow White's esophagus, as walls, fences, trip wires, and bastions were cut away. Another Jericho was crumbling.

The Pacific Northwest summer throbbed with excitement and the games displayed the exhilaration of a true festival. An assortment of Soviet physicians arrived at Sea-Tac Airport to be welcomed by the host families of local doctors. Jan was there. Despite his elation, he felt unusually tense and apprehensive. He hoped his flashbacks would behave. The daily merry-go-round included conference sessions in the Sheraton, followed by excursions to examine advanced medical technology in action. Jan soon warmed to Sergey, a cultured 40-year-old cardiologist from Tbilisi in Soviet Georgia.

Soft spoken, sensitive, and relaxed, Sergey spoke fluent English. Jan took him to observe open-heart surgery and the operation of latest X-ray techniques and CAT scans. They saw art exhibits and ate at the yacht club in Tacoma and Seattle's famous Space Needle. Sergey introduced Jan to a patient from his home town, presently in Seattle for a bone-marrow transplant. For high celebration, he took Jan to a restaurant owned by a classmate from Soviet Georgia—for a genuine Georgian feast. They found they could laugh well together. The only dissonant event was a play about the KGB, and they left the theater long before the conclusion. There were plenty of parties, boisterous drinking and singing, and an unlimited supply of intrigued women.

Despite the terminal condition of her relationship, Renee hosted the family of one of Jan's Soviet new friends. Jan, watching his Esperanza and his friend's child, Katya, splashing merrily together in the Jacuzzi, realized that these two little rascals perfectly symbolized the future synthesis of East and West. Yes, Jan felt an electrifying burst of internationalism well up in his bloodstream. Despite the fears of meeting his old enemies, and his psyche-shaking flashbacks, Jan desperately desired to become part of the growing rapprochement between East and West. He was sure this was where his future would lead him.

The medical metabolism of this first step in the Physicians' Exchange Program was highly productive and exceeded all expectations. Ideas were voiced and plans surveyed for further connections. Both East and West, for example, were engaged in examining the dreadful aftereffects of radiation—the Soviets had Chernobyl, while America had its Hanford "down winders." Proposals were also introduced to develop the resources required to bring Soviet patients to America for treatment.

With the games successfully concluded, Jan was free to expand his Soviet connections and try to resolve his deteriorating family situation. As a natural precipitate of the games, the city of Tacoma seriously considered the idea of asking the city of Vladivostok, the Eastern portal of the Soviet Union, to become its twin city. The timing was propitious, and venturesome plans were hatched at the city council meetings. Later, a group of representatives from many cultural and economic fields would fly over to explore contacts with the city council.

Jan chose his own specific entrance. His attention had been touched by the acute plight of a Vladivostok girl suffering from scoliosis—a severe curvature of the spine. This was a marvelous opportunity for the Tacoma medical fraternity to be of immediate and direct assistance. This, Jan believed, would further help to strengthen the epochal connection between the two cities. Sending his proposals to the chairman of the Executive Committee of the city council, Jan urged him to consider flying the child to America to benefit from the available new treatments. This was a way to harness the residual goodwill of the recent games to a specific humanitarian need. Jan suggested, moreover, that a Soviet team of doctors accompany her to avail themselves of the latest medical techniques, since her care would entail years of protracted treatment. Jan assured the council that a group of local orthopedic experts would contribute their services free of charge. The Soviet doctors could study the new techniques of placing metal rods along the spine with a sequence of tightening devices adjusted over an extended period to bring the spine into correct alignment. In the meantime, the medical fraternity and city would cover all the expenses of little Natalya, her treatment, transport, and care, not to mention the overall expense of the visiting physicians. His letter also expressed Jan's congratulations to the city that planned to celebrate its freedom on January 1, 1991, marking the end of its status as a closed port. To Jan, this startling change presented a tremendous opportunity for friendship. After all, was it not a marvelous covenant of hope that a child should lead the way?

In many respects it was natural for Vladivostok to become Tacoma's twin city. Its global position followed a West to East path, passing from the port of Rotterdam to the port of Tacoma. This line, on a similar latitude, extended across the Pacific to the gateway to Asia. Jan was surprised to discover that all three hubs of commerce, all three ports, were almost 5,100 miles apart from each other. This confirmed for him that his path of destiny was both personally and geometrically aligned.

Vladivostok was a European enclave, an outpost surrounded by Asian territory and consciousness. It was the principal Soviet naval port on the Pacific rim; indeed, its urban persona had been largely shaped by its immensely strategic location relative to the Cold War and the threat from China. It was connected to Moscow by six thousand miles of the Siberian railroad system.

This great port, like Rotterdam and Tacoma, was also filled with fishing fleets, commercial freighters, docks, and food-processing plants. After decades of military restriction and cultural isolation, the city was now poised to break open and inhale the enlivening spirit of the age.

The province, similar in size to Japan and surrounded by vast blessings of barely developed timber and mineral reserves, was handicapped by its lack of technical acumen, equipment, and modern facilities. Its food-processing plants were startlingly antiquated compared to those of the West, while the inefficient methods of harvesting, storage, and transportation perpetuated a wastage the country could ill afford.

The name Vladivostok means "The Preserver of the East." As the sentinel of the eastern approaches, Vladivostok's military persona is clearly declared by numerous statues of military heroes prominently displayed throughout the city and further enhanced by its submarine museum, a gaunt but proud S-56 Guard Red Banner submarine—the "War Glory of the Red Banner Pacific Fleet." Despite its strident military bias, however, the city has retained its own cultural identity. It was a haven for those who had fled the purges so prevalent in Soviet history. Beneath its militant facade lay the latent creative spirit of individualism, its intelligentsia, artists, and thinkers primed for the signal to emerge and regenerate both land and community. As the Soviet Union struggled with its dissolution, so the province became increasingly autonomic. Now its creative juices had begun to enter its bloodstream, despite fears arising from opening the city to the noxious elements of Western society. Despite its residual conservatism, the age of the commissar was now fading. This was the time for arms of friendship to bridge the vast Pacific.

Tacoma's mayor wrote to the Vladivostok council proposing cooperation in urban planning, natural resources economics, transportation, banking, and tourism. Tacoma, she stressed, would gladly support training programs for Soviet businessmen, managers, entrepreneurs—all the energizing elements required for a free-market economy. Her invitation was expansive indeed, for it also proposed the exchange of athletes, educators, and artists.

Jan knew this was the evolutionary moment to look eastwards since the spirit of the age had nodded its assent to the opening of new avenues of fraternity. What better entrance to shared commitment could there be than the care of a child?

As Jan entered the second half of his sixty-third year, so he felt his inner turbulence subside. His psyche was no longer awash with flashbacks. The high waters swamping his composure were dropping, and Jan's sky seemed to lighten towards the East as optimism about his Soviet endeavors lifted the wings of his spirit. His relationship with Renee remained prickly, to say the least, but the lines were now drawn while they awaited the custody settlement. Jan now worked two days a week in his medical office, which gave him time for his projects and his daughter. Yes, Jan felt he was recovering his orientation as the ebbing crisis relaxed its grip.

Then the Persian Gulf War erupted with incredible electronic vividness, and Jan's hard-won composure vanished into the thick smoke of bombardment, his mind suddenly slammed into one tumultuous flashback. He recoiled in horror from this televised theater of the absurd, donated, it seemed, by kind permission of the networks, splintering all semblance of human and divine reason. For hours Jan sat rigidly hunched in his chair, transfixed by the screen, hypnotized by that stricken Baghdad night. What the images neglected, Jan supplied from memories screaming once again in his present. He was there with the children, the mothers, the bewildered soldiers. Enraged by the obscenity of it all, Jan shared the terror of the innocents as Iraq was blasted out of the twentieth century. It was unbelievable! Again, violence begot violence as machines carved the skies, while mortals met their apocalypse. How could the world let loose all this barbaric, brilliant, yet soulless technology of destruction? All Jan could do was thrash about in his nightmare, while denouncing the president and the generals—ashamed of his chosen nationality. Jan condemned the president for his relentless, undiplomatic drive to inevitable conflict. He berated the United Nations for being bought and bribed, while the Soviet veto was self-preoccupied. How could the UN both lose its head and ignore its heart? How could it happen that all the brilliantly innovative faculties of a mustered world intelligence could only choose the bomb and bullet—the most obsolete means available? Were there no creative, non-violent ways to protect the citizens yet still isolate and outmaneuver the ruling clique? Must mankind still slaughter the masses to be rid of tyrants?

For Jan, the desert was a perfect symbol for the present condition of the world's conscience. He was particularly incensed to see the hordes of flag-waving patriots, so proud of a campaign fought with brilliant organization and technology—and use it to purge the guilt of Vietnam. Did they not realize that a nation goes to war when it loses sight of its real mission? Yes, what a magnificent victory of the intellect, and what an abysmal defeat for the human heart and spirit. After all was said and done, it was sophisticated brute force triumphing over ordinary brute force—it was still brute force.

Exhausted by saturation and bleary eyed after hours of compulsive viewing, Jan turned off the screen and stopped the war. But sleep only mocked him while his brain struggled to make sense of it all. Jan wondered if there were millions like himself also manacled to the screen. He wondered if history would even fathom the purpose in it. Was Goethe right when he said that all real wars have a religious foundation to them? As far as Jan could see, the three great religions were locked for eternity in bitter incompatibility. Here they were again, the Star of David, the Monstrance, and the Sickled Moon, that trilogy of tribulation. Would the destiny of the Middle East ever evolve beyong the dark edge of conflict? Would this central stage of destiny ever perform a drama expressing the highest insights and soul powers of humanity? As far as Jan could see, the world's disputes were still subjugated by the archaic law of an eye for an eye, hatred for hatred, vengeance for vengeance, violence for violence.

Jan's night mind's eye pictured the three great religions severed from the transformative juices of spirituality flowing deep in the respective roots of their immense wisdom. Jan, who had a wine glass of Jewish blood in his veins, saw Israel imprisoned in stern and fearful separation, locked in its spirit-paralyzing fear of the Holocaust, using materialism for its solace. He saw it facing the hatred of an Islam now shackled to a materialism born from hydrocarbons, while fuming with the intemperate fires of the jihad.

And where, for goodness' sake, was Christianity? All Jan could detect was its innate impulse of freedom and tolerance being stifled by the rampant materialism occluding the sun radiance of its heart. What a shambles! All Jan could see was antagonism's bloody signature drawn in the sands of Arabian time, spiraling onwards from one historic stage to another. Damn it! There they were again! Those European knights charging the old crusader paths in M-I tanks, chasing that Iraqi mockery of Saladin. Jan saw the flying robes of Lawrence of Arabia charging the Turkish fortress at Akaba, then the shaping of the realm of King Feisal and the birth of Arab nationalism—new states, their ethnic-ignorant frontiers drawn arbitrarily in the sand by European abstraction. How was it that mighty Islam, once the radiant point of high culture, of science, mathematics, and art, had reduced itself to the bartering of oil and weapons? Where was the wisdom in it all?

Had no one listened to the answer, that new path to resolution? Had no one been energized by the immense creative power of the Sermon on the Mount, re-expressed so eloquently by Tolstoy, embodied by Gandhi, and re-formed by Martin Luther King, Jr.? No, those damned dogs of war were true canines, with noses glued to the grounds of expediency. Jan watched the president call for a day of prayer for the coalition forces and their families, but heard no mention of praying for the limbless Iraqi child, the mother crushed by concrete, the simple soldier powerless to change his country, unable to desert a war he could never comprehend, waiting to be obliterated by the Desert Storm. What kind of Christianity was this? What a victory for ice-cold technology. What a defeat for the human spirit.

Under siege from the tangled imagery of screen and flashback, Jan, as usual, struck out into action—at first compulsively so. He got himself into trouble by speaking out at a library storytelling session for mothers and infants.

Unable to stop himself, Jan forcefully urged the startled group to protect the kiddies from trauma by turning off the television set in case they should see mothers engaged in the destructive activities of war, those compelling pictures totally contradicting the feminine archetypes of loving, nurturing, and protecting.

Jan's heavy plea was not appreciated. He was accused of being unpatriotic and told to behave himself in future or be banned. Again, without warning, he spoke up at a church service, stressing the need to protect the children, asking the congregation to set up support services for families with members in the Gulf. But again, Jan's blunt pleadings met embarrassed unease, then cool disdain. Wherever he went, Jan was told his schemes were unrealistic, even crazy, definitely un-American. Jan even made frantic calls to his political representatives in Washington. They listened politely to his suggestions for bringing pressure to bear and recalling all the war mothers from the Gulf. But Jan soon realized this quest was a sheer waste of time. Washington had lost its moral senses. Yes, Jan wanted action, real action, not antiwar rallies yelling for peace then returning home to kick the dog, insult the spouse, and tell the children to be quiet and play with their Nintendo. What a parody!

Jan returned from his forays feeling exhausted and emotionally depleted, but he still had to turn on the screen for the latest war reports. It was the first thing he did, although it only pushed him deeper into his mire of sorrow, leaving him feeling helpless and hopeless, more and more convinced that the war could have been prevented. Jan's German experience reinforced his conviction that every individual must bear the responsibility for this violence, but for the life of him he could not detect the slightest sign of guilt in America at large.

Typically, Jan made his escapes into the mountains or to the coast for quiet times with Esperanza, and these excursions helped settle him a bit. As he regained his centrality and his psychological retort passed from a boiling to a simmering condition, so Jan began earnest and better focused attempts to establish a more logical and attainable project. Synchronous events brought several rather special people into Jan's orbit at this time, and he became increasingly preoccupied with the subject of post traumatic shock syndrome. He enthusiastically availed himself of the new techniques and understanding by attending lectures, meeting veterans who had devoted their lives to it, and by reading profusely. All this was a reflection of Jan's own hospital experience forty-two years previously. Again the past penetrated his present. Jan was shocked to learn that forty percent of those engaged in conflict would suffer from its insidious psychological toxins, not to mention its ever-spreading impact on the metabolism of family life.

Jan's efforts began to change direction and consolidate as he felt more and more compelled to respond to the immediate agony of thousands of Iraqi casualties, now increasing by the hour from the vicious struggle between the desperate regime of Saddam Hussein and the rebellious Shi'ites to the south and Kurds to the north. This was the predictable legacy of the Gulf War, but for the people caught in insurrection it meant disease, chaos, and violence. So Jan tried to find a way to harness the residual goodwill of the Physicians' Exchange Program, hoping to provide medical care for the Iraqi wounded. Tbilisi, in Soviet Georgia, seemed to be a perfect location for a massive treatment center.

As the ideas crystallized, so Jan began drawing the many disparate threads together. He discussed his ideas with local groups and contacted the Red Cross. He also contacted doctors in the Soviet Union and received heartening support from his friend Sergey in Tbilisi. Perhaps they could even involve the veterans of the Vietnam and the Afghanistan wars. Jan also looked for ways to encourage contributions from the large companies who had provided the hideous weapons and munitions of war, and he hoped UNESCO would use its influence. He even enlisted the support of one of the world's leading exports in camp organization.

This was an immense undertaking, by far Jan's greatest challenge, with a vision and scope beyond the wits of one man. But he worked hard, his old fires restoked by meaning, purpose, and urgency. He did what he could and would have to wait for the international fabric of this crusade to weave itself. All Jan could do was help fashion the networking and plan a pilot trip to Tbilisi.

Jan received a telephone call just after returning from his morning jog along the waterfront. His sister in Toronto stated rather tersely that Willem had died peacefully in his sleep during the night. Her brief statement concluded with words clothed in grief and unmistakable frigidity, confirming that Willem had chosen to be interred in Toronto, not with their mother in Tacoma. Jan was given no opportunity to respond.

So, Willem had carried his anger, remorse, guilt, and unforgiveness with him. Letters written before his passage recorded his view that Willem saw his eldest son as nothing more than a crook, a controller, a manipulator of people for his own devices, devoid of any real compassion at all.

Jan winced from the fatality, the abruptness of severance, since his father appeared to be an indestructible resident of time. Jan knew that somewhere in his core he loved this incorrigible enemy; the child in him had always craved for Willem's acceptance. Jan was sure that at least one minute spark of hope for reconciliation had always resisted the storms of ice, although neither he nor Willem had had the gumption to fan it into a useful flame.

His father was ninety, having been thirty when Jan was born. Now the bonds of mortality had released him, and Jan wondered if this season of immortality would compel them both to seek the means of forgiveness in some far-off space and time. The thought of facing family hostility in its concentrated form at the funeral filled Jan with dread, but he decided to go to Toronto and complete their prolonged winter of mutual discontent.

Jan attended the funeral and flew home immediately. None of his children were there, and none of the family members present had anything to say to him. At least he had paid his final respects. Now he had to face his own vexatious litigation squabbles since his relationship lay in the expensive hands of attorneys. Renee, making one last-ditch effort to find a solution, suggested she and Jan live together as a family, on a month's trial. Jan dismissed the opportunity without a thought—his distrust crystallized. He realized there was a chance this litigation could cost him his daughter, which would be the last, fateful straw. Esperanza was Jan's only source of redemption, as he saw it. The court could well become a public arena where he and Renee would parade a bitter litany of reasons why the other was incapable of being fit for custody.

Little Natalya arrived at the Sea-Tac Airport with her retinue of weary, but expectant parents, seven orthopedic specialists, and an advisor. Jan was present to welcome them with the host families, newspaper reporters, and TV cameras. Jan breathed more easily. At least the first stage of this project had gone smoothly. Jan hosted the advisor, a tall, slim, aesthetic-looking Russian in his fifties with a neatly trimmed naval beard. Jan, who considered himself something of a connoisseur of eyes, was immediately touched by Nikolenka's, which were suffused with a mellow warmth and light while being direct and penetrating at the same time. Jan had often thought about the words of Angelus Silesius, who'd suggested that the soul has two eyes, one peering into the mortal world, the other looking into eternity.

As they became better acquainted, Jan was increasingly moved by Niki's rapport with the kingdom of childhood—the natural way he put children at ease. Esperanza soon warmed to Niki's childlike humor, his love of nonsense, particularly his talent for expressing himself in a pictorial and emotive manner. Obviously, he had retained the child in himself. Jan also noticed the unmistakable bond between Natalya and Niki, who stayed with her throughout the harrowing sequence of preliminary spinal examinations, always ready with a smile of affection, a delicate touch, and gentle Russian words of comfort. Niki obviously felt her pain. This was not mere pity, but rather an empathy which poured sustenance into the child's soul. Indeed, Niki carried a subtle air of mystery about him that intrigued Jan. The Russian, however, would never offer personal information unless asked specific questions. His English was remarkably fluent and imbued with the touching charm of an accent.

Jan's days were fully involved with insuring that the whole rescue operation ran smoothly or working on the Tbilisi project. He visited Natalya every day, sometimes taking Esperanza with him, who had recently become increasingly belligerent and uncooperative. Jan wondered if the dreaded family virus of resentment had affected her, too. The more he lavished attention on her, the more resistant and fractious Esperanza became. But things began to alter as Esperanza and Natalya opened to each other. Pale, thin, and in obvious discomfort, the Soviet child glowed when Esperanza brought her books and cuddly things to share. Their friendship flourished despite the language barrier. In fact, Jan's daughter now badgered him incessantly to let her learn Russian. He found a teacher for her while he himself attended language classes at a local university. Soon they were haltingly and humorously conversing at the dinner table with Nikolenka. Jan envied his daughter's natural talent.

Jan and Niki often talked into the early morning hours and he always looked forward to these calming, reassuring conversations. He knew instinctively that he needed something from this unusual fellow. Jan voiced his fears about his impending trip to Vladivostok and Tiblishi; his fear of meeting his old adversaries on their own ground; his fear of the growing political instability as the forces of conservatism, rooted in the pugnacious KGB and military, faced the rising mood of liberalism. Niki offered him an imaginative picture, one perfectly corresponding to Jan's constraining internal conflict.

Niki viewed the rapidly weakening forces of communism as the inevitable release from the repressively dogmatic one-sidedness of Russian masculinity, which had been brutally imposed on the soul of Mother Russia. The innate femininity of the Soviet folk soul, he declared, its aesthetic, devotional, and venerational gifts natural to its being, had been long buried under the debris of scientific and cultural materialism. The intrinsic power of Soviet creativity, he stressed, would emerge as the regenerative energies of reunification—the reunion of Russia's masculine and feminine sides. Niki was convinced that the relief from this paroxysm of history would enable the unraveling Soviet Union to breathe freely again.

Niki went on to emphasize the point that he fully expected a period of trial, dispute, and perilous uncertainty, even chaos, until the two sides of the Russian folk soul found equilibrium. He felt that the present economic decay of both East and West was immensely valuable, a natural consequence, since both had fashioned their economies on militarism. The Soviets had lavished attention on their fear after centuries of barbaric suffering. It was this paranoia that had constructed its fence of missiles. Niki drew Jan's attention to the revitalizing power of warmth engendered by the world's response to the terrible famines of recent years. Suffering had awakened the world's compassion in the form of the massive supplies of food, transport, and expertise flowing into the air and seaports of his homeland. He assured Jan that the people had warmed to such a visible, tangible compassion—things would never be the same again. Niki's complex nation, now splitting into separate nations, would learn to trust again. Yes, he believed the soul of his homeland would open itself to the new millennia with new confidence and less fear.

The farewell party given by the nurses and doctors of the hospital was a clear affirmation of the friendship and bountiful good feelings generated by Natalya's visit. She looked stronger, had more color, and was well able to handle all the fuss being made of her. She now managed to walk a bit each day. Later in Vladivostok, the doctors would continue her treatment, tightening the clamps along the spinal rods bit by bit for several years to come. There were plenty of local doctors, nurses, and administrative staff willing to visit Vladivostok and contribute to the medical work there. Natalya, it was hoped, was the first of many children to visit Tacoma for treatment.

Esperanza and Natalya, now old friends, said their tearful farewells at the airport—Esperanza in Russian, Natalya in English. Esperanza offered her friend a bear carved from a walrus tusk by an Alaskan Indian. Natalya gave Esperanza a beautiful icon in a silver frame. Jan was determined to do anything to bring them together again. He, too, felt a sense of loss when Niki boarded—there was so much he wanted to ask him. No matter, they would meet again soon. Jan would now make ready for his own visit to Tbilisi to join Nicki and Sergey in the Iraq rescue mission.

Chapter V
The Arc of Redemption

The Tiblishi rescue mission accelerated rapidly, with the world's conscience roused by the dreadful plight of a million Kurdish refugees struggling through the mountain snows to reach Iran and Turkey.

The most southern Soviet city, Tiblishi is the major cultural political center in the Republic of Georgia, which sweeps downwards close to the triangle formed by Iran, Iraq, and Turkey. Georgia's fascinating geographical and climatological contrasts rise from the palm-lined coast of the Black Sea, with its vineyards and orchards, up to the fertile highlands guarded by the high ramparts of the Caucasus Mountains. A rugged, majestic land emboldened by mountains yet softened by the sea, Georgia is more Mediterranean in mood than Russian. Its rich, topographical variety is reflected in the fifteen different nationalities living in a land smaller than South Carolina.

Proud of its distinguished hospitality and the independent spirit of its folk soul, the imposing statue of Deda-Kalaki, Mother of the Town, greets the visitor to Tbilisi—with a sword in one hand and a wine cup in the other! The sixth-century steeples of Sioni Church and Cathedral of the Assumption disclose something of the historical dimensions of the city, its orthodox past further underlined by those squat, stubborn sixth-century churches tenaciously rooted in its environs. Georgia's golden age in the twelfth and thirteenth centuries brought forth many monasteries and poets. The rich diversity of its peoples also expressed the innate musicality of the land. Tchaikovsky, for one, spent many years there. The health-provoking properties of the highlands are uniquely evident in the youthfulness of the many centenarians found there. Tbilisi even has a Gerontological Institute to fathom the reasons for their remarkable longevity.

Stalin was one of Georgia's sons. The locals hold a rather ambivalent view of him, detesting his annihilation of the Georgian intelligentsia but grateful for his protection of their living standards. Even before perestroika, Georgians lived better than Russians. They also managed to preserve much of their cultural identity and be more democratic than the other republics—even at the nadir of Soviet stagnation.

Sergey and Niki greeted Jan at the airport and they went straightway to the camp on the outskirts of the city. As their taxi neared the camp located in a huge army base, so the hustle and bustle of the traffic slowed to a walking pace. The camp was still under construction by hordes of workmen and military engineers, while the wounded were being ferried from the airport in ambulances, trucks, and buses. The place was humming with urgency. Everyone had something to do, something to be done quickly. Despite the apparent chaos, the ubiquitous Red Cross and Red Crescent had everything efficiently organized. Most of the doctors, nurses, and medical technicians from Europe, the U.S.A., and Soviet Union were housed in a forest of tents still spreading over the vast grassy areas. The barracks and army hospital housed the wounded. Jan was overjoyed to see the veterans from the Vietnam and Afghanistan conflicts driving buses and trucks, unloading food, medical supplies, and massive crates of advanced equipment. The place was a swirl of directed action, a veritable maelstrom of confounding uniforms, physiognomies, and languages.

Extracting the wounded from strife-torn Iraq was still a problem. But despite the unpredictability of the insurrections, Iranian, Soviet, and Turkish helicopters had continued to nip in and out of the blighted areas and the border refugee camps in Iran and Turkey. The rescue was working. Soon the UN forces would replace the Americans in the protected zone in northern Iraq. Jan saw the afflicted children, young and old people, soldiers, and civilians from the Shi'ite south and Kurdish north. He had seen these injuries before in profusion—the crushed bones, terrible burns, and the ravages of shrapnel. He had, however, never before encountered the ghastly effects of chemical warfare or the severe cases of frostbite inflicted by the perilous mountain crossings.

Jan was deeply moved by the professionally competent dedication of the medical staff and organizers. Here nationalism dissolved in the fire of service. It was a unity formed from a coalescent diversity. The initial, magnesium-like flare of exuberance after the Allied victory in the Persian Gulf had faded rapidly as hearts awakened to the naked aftermath blatantly visible in the heart-wrenching parade of human wreckage. Guilt had fired the will of redemption. This was no place for melancholy sentimentalists.

That first night in Sergey's town apartment, the three of them sat in a pool of exhaustion, absorbing the myriad, gut-twisting impressions of the day. Sergey wondered if war and its terrible consequences would always be a permanent feature of the human milieu. Both he and Jan glanced at Niki, who had said nothing all day. Their friend looked pale and drawn. He answered quietly but with great deliberation and gravity. "I believe humankind must advance—is advancing. It must evolve under the irrepressible thrust of spiritual evolution—the cosmic prerogative. But there is a choice for each human soul, depending on which platform of awareness he or she stands up on. Collision and disaster is one way we engineer our awakening. This is the sleepwalker's entrance to the higher grounds of mindfulness. The other path is free moral choice and action rooted in the higher aspirations of the human soul and spirit—the path of tolerant understanding, goodwill, and communication. It always behooves those working with higher attributes to serve the sleepwalkers who would awaken. They must be taught, guided, loved—not smashed! So war engenders change through suffering. But humanity is not condemned to this tortuous path. Today we saw intelligence, compassion, and empathy directing human skills and strengths in a common cause. Today we saw human hearts responding to a suffering spawned by fear, greed, and power—born in the levels of semi-consciousness."

Sergey and Jan waited for Niki to continue but he did not speak again, and they did not press him. The three of them rested in their thoughts awhile before going to bed. Jan suspected that Niki possessed a profound insight into healing as a spiritual process within the physical. Niki had often talked about it, despite the fact that he had no orthodox medical qualifications whatsoever. During the following days, Jan often caught glimpses of his friend moving about the camp. There was nothing dilatory about Niki's measured tread; in fact, he was the personification of intent. Whatever he was doing, Jan knew Niki was engaged in some manner of service.

Niki would stay awhile in each hospital section. No one ever objected to his presence. Some thought he was a priest of some kind; but even while nurses and doctors were totally absorbed in surgical concentration, they could feel Niki's presence. When possible, Niki would offer a quiet word or two to nurses and doctors. Sometimes he bent over a patient and sank himself into their open eyes. Often he would just stand by the bedside of an unconscious victim, completely composed within himself.

Jan wondered about this kind of mysterious presence. What manner of interior strength coursed through the soul of this man? In some way his quiet friend shared the trauma of each one of them, although Jan could never bring himself to ask about it. It was more a state of being, but one filled with reverence. Yes, Niki carried his ordinariness about him throughout the camp, but it was more of an indefinable super-ordinariness. Jan found himself loving his strange companion without reservation. Through the weeks that followed, Jan realized that Niki carried the suffering of the camp within himself—but freely. He was always at peace with himself. Jan wondered if he himself could ever achieve this incredible equanimity.

Jan and Sergey labored long hours until they felt they would drop—Sergey busy with heart wounds, Jan as a general medical factotum. Their schedules, organized on the shift system, often meant working through much of the exquisite Georgian summer nights. Walking alone along the perimeter fence in the early morning coolness during one of his off-duty breaks, Jan was struck by a mental image of himself working amidst the frenetic haste of the wards, where every drop of human will was directed to the serving of others. He realized that destiny had brought him to this place to serve, yet heal himself. He was simply a servant, yet at the same time soothing, harmonizing, and integrating all those horrific and discordant bits and pieces of his own past. Yes, indeed, Jan was the physician healing himself.

This calming recognition brought a warming sense of thankfulness. Jan doubted if he had ever felt this kind of inner calm. For so long he had survived through the intemperate fire of his will. Now he was sure he felt the effusion of warmth in his soul firmly centered in his heart, totally bereft of the driving, grasping forces of his intellect and will. There were no flames of rage or anger, only the steady presence of glowing embers. It felt so good to feel good.

Three weeks passed in a blur of hyperactivity. The work had gone exceedingly well and countless bodies had been saved. But what about the mending of their minds? Who would care for the psychological aftershocks? Jan agonized over this problem, but it was time for him to return to Tacoma.

That last night the three compatriots, now intimately bonded by their camp experience, feasted, talked, and joked into the night. Jan felt the urge to delve deeper into the mystery of suffering, but the mood was incompatible. Later, however, as the bantering subsided and quietness pervaded the room, Jan reminded Niki that he had briefly mentioned his view of suffering on that first night in Tbilisi. Niki thought for a moment while peering at his own reflection in a large mug of tea he cradled, as he always did, in both hands. Then, looking directly into Jan's eyes, he answered, "All pain is transformative, I believe. Without a meaningful place for suffering in one's inlook and outlook, one can hold no valid philosophy of life. After all, pain is the common property of all. I believe the mission of all destiny is to awaken the organs and faculties of the psyche by experiencing and then assimilating the pain of self and world.

"Pain connects self with self, self to self, self to world. Despite the terror and fear of it, Jan, your pain is your greatest gift to yourself. It is your treasure mined from the motherlode of your mortality. I am suggesting that you suffered because you needed to. I know this is a terrifying thought, but it has made you what you are. It has shaped your destiny, has it not? Likewise, your pain will mold your future and bring you an abundance of fresh opportunity. Through your past agonies, you will eventually deepen and acknowledge your inner realities. You may resist and seek to escape it, that is entirely natural, but it is nevertheless your most immediate form of self-knowing. It is bringing you real cognition, my good friend. As we awaken, so we will require less pain—this is the path to freedom."

In all the time Jan had spent with Niki, he never once heard him reject or judge anyone. Niki would consider the future effects of a person's actions, but he would never impugn or question the integrity of any individual. Similarly, he would never solve another's problems, only energize and nourish the soul who had to face them. If only Jan had met this man years ago.

By early morning Jan was on his way to Washington. He felt different; Tbilisi had changed him. In fact, Jan was certain the Tbilisi camp was the most impressionable experience of his life. His return to Tacoma, however, immediately brought him down to earth. In an instant Jan dropped from an intense transpersonal experience onto the plane of his personal dilemmas.

The custody hearing went remarkably quickly and was surprisingly amicable. Renee was given custody, but Jan received rather liberal visitation rights, which included taking his daughter to Russia for limited periods after she was twelve. His generous financial settlement was not contended.

Esperanza was now a rather delicately built seven year old, nimble and fleet of foot, a natural dancer perhaps. Mentally sharp, she was quick to grasp the essentials, particularly in languages that she loved. Her sleep patterns, however, were irregular, and her intermittent nervousness gave rise to concern. Esperanza's attention tended to dart from one thing to another and weakened her attention span. Her health was sound, except for a tendency to develop ear infections. In general, Esperanza was a precocious child and unusually comfortable around adults.

Renee continued her role of protector, while Jan persisted in taking his daughter to any event he thought would please her. Whatever the harmful results of living in the tension of opposites might be, Esperanza would have to transmute them later on through the power of her own emergent personality.

Renee and Jan searched for a mutually acceptable school for Esperanza, one which would respond to her natural creativity and foster the all-round process of her development. They concurred on the choice of the local Rudolf Steiner school. Jan knew that these schools were also opening in the eastern bloc countries—there was even one in Vladivostok. Jan equated this particular philosophy of education with freedom. He knew that one of Hitler's early decisions after taking power was closing down all the Steiner schools, which later were the first schools reopened by the American forces of occupation.

This education, he and Renee believed, was a rare sanctuary of childhood, one placing devoted emphasis on the development of Esperanza's will, emotional expansion, and intellectual awakening, in stages following the developmental passage of childhood. As far as they could determine, it was the most universal education they could find to help prepare Esperanza for a life of personal meaning and purpose. Here, the rich wisdom inherent in myths and history would foster her global awareness and her acceptance of human, cultural, and historical differences. Here was a creative blend of science and art. Thus Renee and Jan hoped that Esperanza's natural wonder would not be suppressed but be nourished to form the foundation for her journey of self and world discovery. They hoped she would awaken the inner capacities and faculties necessary to live a life of personal and social meaning in a new millennia, teeming with dangers, dispersions, opportunities, and challenges. They believed this approach would address the needs of Esperanza's body, soul, and spirit. Above all, it would recognize her uniqueness as being sacrosanct.

Jan flew into the major Pacific coast airport at Khabarovsk and was warmly welcomed by Nikolenka and a delegation from the Vladivostok City Council. Later that day, he and Niki strolled down the wide and clean Leninskaya Street. The architecture of most of the buildings in the inner city was typical of the early years of the century. Jan was amazed to see how visually close it was to being the twin of Tacoma, except for the sparse traffic and lack of pollution. They rode in a trolley bus down to a harbor jammed with ships from all over the world. They walked along the waterfront past the memorial sign erected in honor of the city founders, its elegantly simple form sweeping upwards to a pinnacle. There were plenty of sailors around to remind Jan that this was still a military harbor. The locals looked relaxed, moving at a mere fraction of the American street bustle. The city center was clean and pleasant with numerous parks and attractive flower beds.

Niki lived in a two-room apartment in one of the blocks of rather new high-rise apartments overlooking the ocean. His living room revealed another aspect of his unusual character—books. All the free wall space was jammed with books from floor to ceiling. There were books on religion, mythology, world history, a whole wall of western books in German, Spanish, French, and English. *Where did he get them all?* Jan wondered. One wall welcomed all the masters of Russian literature. Jan knew some, but there were plenty he had never heard of. He noticed the wide selection of Christian works, ranging from the orthodox to the esoteric. All these volumes were extremely well worn. Apparently, Niki's intellectual colleagues used his home as a library. They did not talk that first night; Jan was too exhausted from the long flight.

Jan woke up early, anxious to prepare himself mentally for the council meeting. Niki cooked him a good American breakfast to start the day before they took the trolley to the modern, twelve-story Executive Committee building with its lion-crest panel prominently displayed on the ramparts.

Jan sat nervously through the customary Soviet speeches expressing the city's gratitude for Natalya's treatment, stressing the hope that more children could go to the Pacific Northwest for treatment, especially the leukemia patients. Apparently, everyone in the city knew about Natalya, now something of a local celebrity and doing well. Then it was Jan's turn to present his proposals, a long drawn-out procedure because of the intervals needed for the interpreter. Jan proposed a list of ideas for consideration, including regular physician exchange programs, arrangements for taking more sick children to Tacoma, the setting up of CAT-scan equipment in Vladivostok, regular half-yearly conferences, and design support for a major housing complex complete with medical clinics, based largely on Jan's old Seattle plan. His drawings and charts were shown on the wide screen and the meeting concluded. Questions would be asked on another day.

Jan felt totally drained. Talking always wearied him, and he hoped the interpreter had injected a little life and inspiration into the translation. His spirits, however, revived in the evening when Nikolenka brought him a bottle of vodka and the warmth of his personal attention. The convivial mood, encouraged by the alcohol, loosened Jan's tongue and he told Niki the story of his early life and his relationships; the whole sorry tale came pouring forth. Niki said nothing, allowing Jan's pent-up tension to fully exhale itself.

Jan, in turn, had been dying to know something about Niki's background, since there had been little opportunity to do this in Tbilisi. Niki obliged and went back as far as his grandparents, who were Tolstoyians. They had loved the old aristocrat cum peasant, and had later joined one of the numerous Tolstoyian communes springing up throughout the world. His grandfather had even met Lev Tolstoy in Yasnaya Polyana, the Tolstoy estate near Moscow. Niki's grandfather was one of the multitude making the pilgrimage to bask in the aura of the old rebel, whose power at that time rivalled that of the czar. Niki's grandfather had found Lev in a petulant mood, grumbling profusely about all the spice cakes for the guests, while peasants were starving all over Russia. His grandfather had often spoken fondly of Tolstoy, describing his long, tangled beard, the remarkable clarity of his eyes; Lev dressed like a muzhik and strode about in boots that he had made himself. Niki's father, a professor in Leningrad when the Bolsheviks swept the academic stage free of independent thinking, was a deeply religious man, a student of history and world religions. Naturally, he soon fell afoul of the purges by publicly denouncing the university's loss of academic freedom. He died in one of Stalin's gulags.

Niki paused for a moment, perhaps savoring a precious recollection or a sense of loss. His mother was still well and active and living in Vladivostok. She had long ago chronicled all the details of her husband's mock trial and persecution. Only now, in the shifting political climate, could she bring herself even to contemplate retrieving her manuscript from its hiding place.

Niki himself had struggled for years to bring innovative ideas to his hospital and its social services. He was a qualified counselor. He had been severely ostracized for not being a party member, and the KGB had kept tabs on him for years. Jan asked Niki how he found the strength to breathe so freely in a society reeking of restriction? How did he avoid being turned in for possessing all these Western books? How did he manage to teach, to develop his numerous educational initiatives? Niki answered with his own questions. "How," he asked, "can anyone engage the sustaining and enlivening forces within their own psyche? How can anyone remain open to the crushing travail of the world without being morally brutalized?" Niki answered his own inquiry by stating that the only answer for him was daily meditation, contemplation, prayer, and study. Only this way could he draw upon his own interior resources of strength, creativity, and affirmation. Only this way could he convert his pain and fear into understanding and capacity for living. He could nourish himself only by drawing on the inexhaustible power of his own spiritual life. This was the only path to interior freedom Niki could find.

Niki then gently shifted the conversational focus by drawing Jan's attention to the fact that Jan's history, so it seemed to him, was shaped largely by forces of compulsion and reaction—those persistent energies that had dominated and then wrecked Jan's relationships and peace of mind. Niki suggested that only by awakening and courageously facing his inner life could Jan ever hope to learn how to forgive, yes, even love those who had hurt and persecuted him. These were direct and unexpected comments. Jan felt himself contract for a moment, but then the softness of Niki's voice, completely free from any hint of moral indignation, enabled him to exhale. Jan knew this man loved him, regardless of everything and anything.

Aware of Jan's reflexive reaction, Niki again shifted his emphasis to a broader, though compatible, scene. He believed that the emergent new nations would offer a new kind of conscience to the world. The people, he stressed, had a unique sensitivity, a long preoccupation with the nature of good and evil. "Look at its writers," Niki pointed to the lines of Russian wisdom on the book shelves, "particularly Tolstoy, Dostoevsic, Soloviev. I firmly believe the Russian folk soul will eventually awaken its new spiritual identity and pour it into the destiny of the new millennia. Buried deep beneath the collapsing edifices of materialism are the roots of Russian destiny, which will further uncover the mysteries of good and evil and discover new ways to live. Tolstoy concentrated on the moral transformation of the soul, but the new age will seek to spiritualize the life and work of the world. Yes, the love mystery is central to this irrepressible quest in Russian destiny. With its sages, musicians, artists, and writers, and the countless religious impulses emerging from the musty catacombs of repression, Russia will revive its spirit after decades of slumber and moral decadence."

Jan knew that this was a precious opportunity for his questions. He might not have the chance again since so many people demanded Niki's personal time. He suspected his friend had cleared a space just for him, and he was grateful. Jan had recognized Niki's love for history. He obviously saw more than dates, disasters, and triumphs in it; he saw it as more than one-damn-thing-after-another history. So Jan asked Niki what he saw behind the chaotic tumult of events.

After a customary pause for reflection, Niki answered, "For me, history reveals humankind's relentless march towards individuality. At the expense of the old unconscious, symbiotic unity, humankind has separated itself into smaller and smaller groups until left with the harrowing loneliness of the individual core. History, to me, looks like mitosis in reverse! It is a relentless odyssey of separation until the unique ego stands nakedly exposed to its own consciousness, and this is the point of it all—until now."

Jan inhaled every word. He yearned for an overview of life, after floundering among the surface troughs and crests of history making for so long. He had been abused by it. Now Jan needed to understand it. There was no brainwashing here. On the contrary, Niki always insisted Jan not accept anything offered on blind authority but always rock new ideas in the cradle of contemplation, and examine carefully before rejection, acceptance, or storing for another time.

Niki built on his theme, "The route to true selfhood is a narrow and dangerous climb. The waking mind is prey to egoism and all its divisive progeny—everything from the enticements of self glorification to the paralysis of cynicism and nilihism. All this is just part of the trek, the spiritual homelessness while stumbling through the forest of experience. This is the pain of the age—the pain of the Western psyche, particularly. But only on this path can mankind acknowledge the reality of selfhood and its rights to independent freedom."

Then Niki shifted gears, his words imbued with more intensity. "But this point is only a beginning. A new road winds through the millennia ahead. Now the hard-won, independent self must strive to reintegrate itself with humanity by evolving new, ever flexible social forms and levels of human rapport, which will allow this individuality to express itself in freedom. This is why the modern soul yearns to recover unity and belonging, without, however, sacrificing one mite of its moral freedom and awakening cognition. Essentially, it leads to a more profound way of loving.

"Jan, just look at the trauma being enacted on the world stage at this very moment. Observe how the exalted wisdom of the East cries out for a path to completion and union. Its colossal spirituality is an incomparable gift, but it is blocked and will become degenerate unless it can find a way to acknowledge the immortal uniqueness of the single human self. Without a living perception of the spiritual evolution of self, world, and universe, it is doomed to rot in its socks. The Western mind, on the other hand, dominated by its fierce drive for individuality and independence, bewitched by the material universe, the Hansel and Gretel candy house, has sacrificed its connection to the deep springs of its spirituality. See how its soul shivers and thirsts for personal meaning. This is why East meets West in the Middle East—the historical stage of catharsis—the clashing place of old dogmas, institutions, and mentalities. No wonder fire and ice create so much moral and rhetorical steam!"

Jan questioned Niki's use of the word "morality," since he himself had tangled with a couple of ethics committees and it had left a bad taste in his mouth; indeed,

Jan had always had a sticky time with this word. His friend nodded but rose to stretch his legs, suggesting they brew another pot of tea and turn on the lights. Neither of them had really noticed the night nestling around them. Later they resettled themselves in the comfortable Ukrainian chairs and sipped their tea. Jan felt physically tired but never had he felt more mentally receptive.

Jan looked at his companion. He had grown so accustomed to Niki, as if he had known him all his life. He noticed the flecks of gray streaked among the light brown hair at the temples, the color more prevalent in Niki's short beard. Niki's expressive nose, suggestive of the man's ability to feel things deeply, reminded him a bit of Ralph Waldo Emerson's. He certainly had Emerson's gentleness of soul. For a man totally dedicated to individuality, Niki had not a selfish fiber in him. His goodness might be threatening if it were not for his unpretentious simplicity and humility. He had eyes and ears like everyone else, but these eyes really looked, and Niki's ears really listened.

Niki spoke. "Time and time again today, I hear people say, 'It's not an ethical problem. We need a practical, commonsense, pragmatic solution. It's no good confusing the issue with morality.' Yes, I've heard it countless times in medical, commercial, and political conversations. But I have come to believe that *all* the world's dilemmas—personal, national and global—are essentially moral issues. Yes, I do believe that everything to do with man and the universe is immersed in a deeper moral reality. Anything to do with choice has a moral significance. We can't have real freedom without using moral imagination, courage, and responsibility. Morality is much more than a habit, doctrine, or fashion; it lies at the very heart of human evolution.

"We, perhaps more than other people, have dimly intuited that both individual and nation are arenas where moral and immoral forces battle for dominance. In fact, this antagonism has always been the source of our suffering; our people have always struggled to unravel the moral essence of things. You can hear this in our music and sense it in the works of men like Tolstoy, Dostoevski, and Pasternak. Look for it, too, in our modern artists. Yes, we have always had a lover's quarrel with our moral dilemmas. It is part of our covenant with destiny. Tearing ourselves free from the stifling amorality of communism gives us a tremendous opportunity for awakening our moral conscience. Yes, we will re-plough the poisoned ground. Perhaps you can see this, too, as America's greatest source of social confusion.

"The primitive, still experimental forms of democracy sleepily stretching themselves in the morning sun will never unfold their immense gifts and recognition of the rights of the authentic self if shut off from their moral blood streams. Morality is not a straitjacket of 'thou shalt nots.' You cannot legislate it unless it is felt, thought, and willed as a personal impulse working in motive, choice, and action. This is why I devote my heart to education. This is where we can nourish the emerging powers of imagination and energetic feeling and thought. This is now the church of churches. This is where hope resides—in the young souls of the new age. At one stage of evolution it was correct to say that what is true for one may not be right for the other. But one fine, conscious day it will be right to say what is right for one is right for all others. In a nutshell, Jan, I am suggesting that the spiritual evolution of humanity and morality are inseparable. It is not a philosophical problem. It is present in the immediacy of making choices and living each day well."

Jan and Niki sipped and talked through the dark hours until the first thin edge of dawn squeezed itself between the black bars of sea and cloud. What a remarkable night it had been—and not a single yawn. Over the years, Esperanza, in her early years, had led Jan into the luminous world of fairy tales and myths. Suddenly he realized he, too, had encountered the wise man of the woods, the hermit in the cave, the old woman, the birds that talk, those who wait to guide the questing soul along its path. He understood. Every Parsival will meet them. But he had waited so long. No matter, Jan had found his own guide, and he knew he would never lose his way again.

Jan asked Niki one final question as the first bird song touched the ear of the new day. He asked Niki if he could help him plan a period for meditation, contemplation, and prayer. Niki was delighted and outlined the basic steps, knowing full well how difficult it would be for a man so dominated by outer action. But he trusted the wisdom of Time, hoping Jan would strenuously try to direct his powerful will inwards as well as outwards. Jan, who had never found any access to sustained peace, decided to build a period of fifteen minutes meditation into the structure of each day.

Jan and Niki attended the council meetings the following three days, where each of Jan's proposals were scrutinized intently. They were certainly no pushovers, these shrewd and down-to-earth Russians. The council decided, however, to appoint a task force of experts with diverse skills to fly to Tacoma to develop each of the initiatives further. Niki remained silent during these sessions, but Jan felt the infusion of Niki's strength sustaining him. Jan was thankful, so much had gone well so far. Everything would take time, he realized.

Jan flew on to Tbilisi to meet Sergey and attend an international symposium devoted primarily to the knotty problems of medical ethics, covering, among other things, genetic engineering, abortion, and euthanasia. Being among physicians and delegates from over two hundred countries gave Jan a distinct and refreshing sense of being not a Dutchman or an American but rather one of the new planetarians Niki and his friends had talked about so enthusiastically.

Sergey, ever the fun-loving Georgian, hustled Jan from one thing to another—the port, theaters, museums, restaurants—until Jan's legs and stomach begged for mercy.

Back in Tacoma, Jan labored on six different committees. He persuaded his son Theo to represent him and connect with Vladivostok architects working on Jan's now highly modified Seattle plan. He even managed to draw his eldest son Diaz into the program, since Diaz's expertise on immigration law was of immense value now large numbers of Russians and Americans were leaping the Pacific. Jan was delighted. Hopefully, all his children would align their lives with the emergent fervor of internationalism. Nothing would make Jan happier (except their acceptance of him as a father), viewing him not as a man submerged in error and misjudgment, but one striving to transmute his past, struggling to fulfill destiny in the midst of others also demanding their right to grow. Would they *ever* forgive him? Could they ever transform their bitterness? Would they find a Niki? If only Jan could find a way to communicate with them, but he knew he lacked the art, the skills, to bridge the chasms cut by the old rivers of his children's distrust.

The months passed swiftly, and Jan's condominium was now seldom without Russian visitors. Indeed, Tacoma now possessed a distinct Russian flavor. There were Russians everywhere, students in the colleges and hospitals, soccer and ice hockey teams at the Tacoma Dome, Russian art in the galleries, Russian plays in the theaters. The Russian spirit revitalized and enriched both the culture and the commerce of the northwest, which had recently formed its own common market of the Pacific Rim. The same was true in Vladivostok, where the free-market economy inspired new optimism and confidence after the gloom of the second great economic depression had lifted. Both nations had adjusted painfully to economies no longer fed by the old military complexes. Symposiums and cooperative research programs now abounded on both sides of the Pacific. Jan had recently attended one on medical ethics and genetic engineering. Soon he would join a Tacoma delegation at an East-West conference grappling with urban development, crime, and addiction.

Jan studiously kept his daily meditation routine, no matter what the demands on his time and energy. This early morning ritual became a special time for him. As the months passed, Jan increasingly felt its benefit, finding himself in closer contact with the inner source of his confidence. He could think more clearly, intuit more directly, be less impulsive and reactive. He could better sense the reality of others, not his own reactions to them. Yes, Jan's emotional self was undoubtedly freed from upsurges and downswings. Consequently, he was more at ease with himself and others. Slowly, Jan managed to face his past and its taunting ghosts of shame and guilt. Whenever he felt the old dragons gnawing at his psyche, he called Niki. Yes, Jan was sure he detected signs of inner change. Some kind of interior transformation was at work. His flashbacks had long since disappeared.

It was clear to Jan also that the world's soul, likewise, was grinding its way through another of its great metamorphoses. The scattered violence in the highly agitated and now independent republics had subsided with the experimental formation of the new commonwealth. There were myriad ethnic controversies to be ironed out, but the overall concept had met general approval.

As the new European community gained the cohesion of political, cultural, and economic unity, so it became the natural fulcrum in the dynamic interplay of East and West. China's inertia sustained its doctrinal vacillation as it reluctantly shuffled its way into the new millennia, but it had applied to join the new Pacific Rim organizations. To do this, it would have to open its doors wider. The destiny of India was still preoccupied with the volatile tensions between Muslim and Hindu, and the thorny antagonists in the Middle East continued to present the imagination, ingenuity, and patience of the New World mind with strenuous exercise. The predilection for brinkmanship in the past decades, amply supported by a procession of crotchety dictators with large bank accounts and small minds, kept the world on its toes. Fortunately, the worldwide limitation on arms sales kept their wings clipped. The cyclic melodrama of the Middle Eastern peoples, obdurately holding on to their ancestral suspicions, continued to rattle the equanimity of the world mind, but the Palestinian nightmare was now hopefully put to flight by the donation of land by Israel, Jordan and Iraq.

To Jan, so much of history was a mirror image of his own life problem—forgiveness and cohesion versus separation and conflict. Jan, however, was hopeful. The revitalized intelligence of the United Nations was now better equipped to temper the hot-blooded regional antagonists through its economic, military, and political pressures. The rapid development of the Russian oil fields, together with alternative energy sources, had weakened the ransoming power of the Arabian states.

Perhaps, Jan mused, the world mind had learned a few lessons after all, being less inclined to superimpose its concepts on communities making their own arduous way to higher levels of political awareness. Thankfully, there was now more respect for the unique developmental processes working within the different societies. As the East-West line of culture stabilized, so it could release energy to assist the Third World in enhancing its quality of life and allow it to pour its own unique cultural energy into the world chalice. The rising involvement in conservation and pollution control heightened the sense of viewing the earth as a whole. This new holism now had to face the staggering challenge of a degenerating global ecosystem and the stricken quality of life in the vastly overpopulated Third World nations. The planet was too human-heavy and the growing use of these growing reservoirs of labor by the technological civilizations put severe economic stress on their own peoples.

Jan and Niki loved to walk along the headland at sunset and befriend the lonely lighthouse looking out into the vastness of the Pacific. These were special times for them both, when their conversation touched deep levels of mutuality. On one occasion, Jan expressed his sense of excitement, convinced he now saw more peace than conflict, both in his own life and in the world at large. Niki, however, fell silent for a moment of introspection before expressing some of his deepest concerns. Then he countered

Jan's exuberance with words of warning. "I believe the forces of future conflict are already germinating in every cell of human activity and aspiration, forces that will undoubtedly push the global soul into new cycles of disparity. The source of this growing separation and turmoil is deeply embedded in the struggle between belief and unbelief—the mounting antagonism between the mechanistic, materialistic concepts of life and emerging insight into the wider spiritual reality behind humanity, earth, and universe.

"One can hear the call to arms in the fields of education, medicine, ethics, and law. Science, which examines the mystery of life from a purely biochemical and corporeal standpoint, is directly opposed to the idea that nonphysical processes lie behind every activity in the physical universe. This sharpening dichotomy is increasingly evident everywhere one looks. Both have their own view of the laws of cause and effect. Education, in particular, is the primary arena of conflict—and will be for a long time. The essential battle is the struggle for the allegiance of the single human soul."

Niki went on to voice another concern. "The growing disenchantment with government and political integrity in the eighties and nineties, combined with the staggering advances in communication, have conjured forth the phantasmagoric power of the 'public mind.' This mass mind now imposes its own form of tyranny by manipulating people's emotions and doing their thinking for them. The declining virility of education and the corresponding rise of mediocrity is particularly dangerous. Only a revitalized education dedicated to awakening the innate faculties of the individual psyche can erase this pervasive threat. To do this means awakening to the spiritual nature of the individual and its development stages.

"Another thing irritating the oyster of the new millennium is those scattered outbreaks of infectious nationalism which always seem to manifest themselves when the resistant forces of the old encounter those of the future. Nationalism was once perfectly valid, a necessary phase in social evolution, but now it is rendered obsolete as humanity moves towards a sense of global humanitas. Nationalism separates, emphasizes, and hardens differences. It seeks to disconnect one people from another."

The two friends strolled back from the lighthouse without further talk, as a chilly sea breeze sprang up to match Niki's sobering comments.

The following day was a Sunday, and Jan rose earlier than usual to make coffee and take a cup to his friend's bedroom. He placed the steaming mug on Niki's bedside table and noticed a strikingly beautiful gold and silver filigree frame holding a photograph of a woman—probably taken in her early thirties. Her slightly angular features, short dark hair, and engaging smile reminded Jan of Edith Piaf, the popular French singer, affectionately known as the "Little Sparrow." Jan knew Niki had once been married. His friend, however, had never revealed anything about his wife. Jan had watched Niki's relaxed manner with his numerous female friends, not to mention the many attractive doctors and counselors at the hospital. He was sure Niki had no current romantic attachments—and he wondered why.

Jan envied Sergey, who glowed in the presence of those provocative Georgian beauties. Sergey had been married three times already and would probably sustain the pattern. Women appeared to be a vital ingredient in his irrepressible lust for life. They responded to the magnetic charm of his subtly sensual nature.

Jan mused on his own romantic episodes, all those warm, fresh thermals of anticipation lifting him heavenwards, only to drop him onto the frozen ground of disappointment. He winced from the thought that his own children viewed him as a feckless womanizer. Could he ever break the cycle of flames to ashes? How had Niki fared? He resolved to ask Niki about his wife.

Later that evening, after Niki's young literary friends had left, Jan ventured his question. The mood was perfectly sympathetic since the evening discussions were centered on the psychological relevance of the Tristan and Isolde myth. Niki obliged and spoke with words touched with both warmth and tender sorrow. "Natasha? We met at the university while studying education. We were both nineteen years old." He then rose to fetch her photograph from the bedroom and placed it on the coffee table, where he and Jan could both look at it.

"Actually, it was old Tolstoy himself who brought us together. As you know, he spent a lifetime wrestling with the man-woman mystery. In fact, it is the major theme in all his novels. Natasha had discovered one of his little books on education describing his small village school at Yasnaya Polanya. She asked our professor if he knew anything about Tolstoy's approach to childhood. You know, Tolstoy loved children, and instinctively understood them. Yes, I remember those moments in the lecture hall so vividly. Natasha was blessed with a natural enthusiasm for the world of ideas. She would hold them like gemstones, turning them in the light, looking at them through every facet. Her mind was so fresh and open, yet also imbued with feminine intuition. She was interested in everything. Well, our dour, gray-suited lecturer knew about Lev Tolstoy. He peered over his spectacles and tersely dismissed him as being irrelevant. Tolstoy had nothing pertinent to contribute to the party's view of modern education. I felt so saddened to see Natasha's genuine interest doused by an answer that was more of a reprimand. Despite my shyness, I decided to introduce myself after class and tell her about my grandparents' connection to the Tolstoyians."

Niki shifted his eyes from Jan to the photograph. "It was the strangest thing, Jan. Despite our individualistic natures, it was as if we already *knew* each other. There was nothing to overcome, no need to peel away the painful onion skins of our personas to touch the essence of each other. It sounds unbelievable, but it seemed as if all this had been worked out long before we met. Even the sorrow of being unable to bear children could not threaten our certainty of each other nor the harsh political persecutions we had endured in our early twenties. This mutual trust and confidence meant that the blessing of our marriage could flow outwards to others and, indeed, many souls were drawn to us. This helped me to overcome my monastic nature and respond to others.

"Was she perfect? Far from it. I did not idolize her, I loved her. She was a scramblehead! Ideas were forever tumbling around in her mind—a veritable washing machine! She had trouble organizing all this mental activity. What a confusion Natasha would get herself into—especially with practical things like shopping lists, financial affairs, and birth dates. But I loved her because of it and we laughed and giggled our way through so many embarrassing mix-ups. I even introduced her to Aristotle's logic and set her daily exercises to direct her will and bring some structure into her cerebral whirlpool." Niki laughed, "I remember us once rushing out of a crowded station—talking as usual. Natasha got caught up in the crush and went through the door ahead of me talking to the stranger beside her—about Plato! And guess what? He was the KGB agent who had been assigned to watch our movements that week! I wish could have seen his befuddlement! How we laughed!

"Yes, Jan, we learned much, quarrelled never, and loved always. Natasha taught me to open my heart and respond to others, to cherish the gift of the moment, to play with the child in me. Through her, I eventually shed my mantle of shyness with people. One can't be a real educator without an expressive connection with the child and youth within oneself. Yes, we were two become one; one become two. I have never forgotten a quote from one of your Sioux Indians. 'The path through life is exceedingly narrow. Two may only travel as one.' Does it all sound unbelievable, Jan?" Jan nodded and Niki continued. "There was not a scrap of marshmallow sentimentality about it. We felt our marriage was indeed a sacrament—bestowed by grace, a gift we had to share with others. Not only were we soulmates, we were spiritmates as well." Niki dropped his eyes—and his smile. "But it could not last. She died when we were thirty-five."

Niki interlaced the fingers of both hands and peered into the hollow within. "Despite our preparations, the finality of separation cast me into an abyss. I felt frozen in a cocoon of gloomy nothingness. You see, Jan, I was so sure our connection would continue in some form. A few weeks before Natasha's departure she pledged herself to uphold our work wherever she was in her postmortem existence. Surely, she would slip gently into my dreams to guide me. Surely, I would sense her dear presence when walking through our favorite woods. Surely, our love would find a way to bridge the great divide. But nothing happened! All I could sense was my forlorn emptiness. My soul was torn from me. I couldn't even raise the power to continue my inner work. All study, prayer, and contemplation seemed utterly useless. I lived like a robot for many months."

When Niki fell silent, Jan glanced back over his own wake of emotional deaths. He felt he had, indeed, caught the ethereal fragrance of the eternal woman in each of his women for a fleeting moment before it was swept away by the storms of personality. Yes, he had been left with so many romantic bereavements. All these graves were inscribed with the same words: "Woman, the enigma."

Niki resumed his story. "Natasha succumbed to leukemia. Nothing much could be done except for two years of spiritual preparation when we read everything we could find about the idea of immortality." He smiled, "But you know, Jan, we are closer now than we were then." He nodded to himself. "I began dimly to sense her nearness soon after I resumed my meditation in my efforts to reconnect myself to my own hibernating soul life. I found her there! Perhaps Natasha had waited there all the time. Yes, my friend, I know that I know she still invests her love in me. Her guiding presence is a daily reality for me. The marriage holds! This will sound odd to you, but I still try to help her by reading aloud from the Gospels, the Bhagavad Gita, Rudolf Steiner's lectures on the journey between death and rebirth—even a bit of Aristotle now and then to keep her organized! I feel no pain, no dimming of her beauty, no sadness for my loss of physical comfort and companionship. Natasha and I are still together. Perhaps she can even guide me better from where she is."

Niki sank back into his chair, and Jan again looked over his own collection of paradoxical images of woman. Yes, he had gloried in the enveloping comfort of surrender. But all too soon, the flush of love decomposed into the heart-lost disengagement of sex, his love churned into discontent by the relentless mill of his vulnerability.

Niki intervened, as if reading Jan's thoughts. "Jan, I am sorry your picture of woman is so painfully fractured. I do realize that my words have lifted some fresh pain from old memories. But can you see that all your women were Natashas? Were they not your teachers, instructing you in the matters of the soul? They wished to love you, not torment you. Perhaps they tried to change you, but they really wished to awaken you. If they tried to change you, they invited their own lessons of pain, but they offered their unique gifts to you nevertheless—as best they could. And you did learn from them, Jan. You do carry your Natashas with you. You have received their gifts, although you may not recognize them. But you will. You eagerly sought outwards for love, but your Natashas turned you back towards your own soul—your relationship to yourself. When all is said and done, this was largely their mission."

Although it was close to midnight, Niki and Jan felt the need to stretch their limbs and breathe the fresh night air. They walked down the hill and through one of the city parks. The lights were out and the place was deserted, but the path was dimly lit by a declining moon to the west.

Both of them were occupied by their contemplations. Jan wondered what his friend had meant by the veiled suggestion that Niki had known Natasha before they met each other.

He and Niki sat for a while on a dew-coated bench. How different everything looked at this hour, so free from distractions, the close environment formed by impenetrable shadows, ghostlike diffusions, and subtle fragrances.

Niki had often dropped vague hints about the idea of reincarnation, but he had never directly declared himself.

Jan decided to tackle him on it, but as usual, Niki answered questions by asking them—his favorite form of verbal engagement. "Let me ask you, Jan, can you detect any sign of an all-pervading justice behind the world's life? If not, how can you truly live without it, unless you close your eyes to the almost impenetrable blanket of suffering, smothering humanity? What about the deaths of babies in the genocidal floods ravaging Bangladesh? The earthquakes in Armenia? The stunted hope of the children in the Sudan? Why should we suffer these perils of existence?

"I ask you, can you content yourself with but one erratic flutter in mortal time? Here you are, your age leading into the lush foothills of wisdom, but soon you will be left without the opportunity to put it to good account. Your life is filed under the name 'Experience,' but what can you do with that bulging document? Did you play the roulette wheel of birth, which brought you to the glorious birth of a new millennium? Why were you not born in a fading Stone Age tribe in New Guinea? What makes you so special?

"What about those poor souls crushed under the hooves of Mongol invaders long ago? Is history merely a tale told by an idiot? How can humanity advance if every soul starts with an absolutely clean slate? Were all your talents embedded by chance in your DNA, or are you the eclectic product of your environment? Did you bring *nothing* at all with you for your journey? Is not the word *destiny* a useless, empty shell without a before and an after? Where is the justice? What about the poor soul doomed from birth by brain damage, totally dependent on others? What about the soul enduring years of struggle with multiple sclerosis? What about the spinster sacrificing all hope of marriage and independence by caring for an aged parent? Where lies the reason?"

Niki waited for the questions to sink in. But Jan had barely begun to adjust to them when Niki pushed on. "Jan, how high can you climb in one brief life? Are you then doomed to play a secondary role in celestial affairs in some obscure corner of the universe? Why strive and suffer for perfection? Why try to change the world in one brief mortal fling? Does the wall of death block all your avenues of growth? What will you do with all those painful life lessons you have learned? What happens to all your angers, wishes, intentions, and guilts? And what about love? Have you surrendered all hope? How can you enlarge your being and correct your errors in just one narrow slice of time? How came you to be shoved into the Russian front? How came you to America? To this bench? Where are the *real* causes? Are we ruled by a highly skittish creator with a spooky sense of humor? Or are you, as the mechanists insist, a brief and random assemblage of genetic fates?" Niki stopped abruptly leaving Jan completely stranded. But then he added an afterthought, "Whatever you believe, in one or many lifetimes, it must satisfy reason—it must be reasonable."

They walked back up the hill, Jan musing on his own astonishment. Life had so many hidden dimensions. There was so much to examine.

Later that year, Jan celebrated his seventieth birthday in Tacoma, and for the first time in decades at least four of his six children shared it with him, which gave him much pleasure. A few months earlier Jan had been jolted into sensing his own mortality by the first signs of a heart condition. This intrusion into his hard-won equilibrium sent Jan's spirits into a tailspin. At first he was angry. How dare his robust constitution let him down now? There was so much work to be done, so much to learn. Many of Jan's projects were nearing completion, and his calendar was plastered with notations—countless impending visits and meetings.

But the crisis passed; Jan's difficult withdrawal from activity was supported by his inner work and regular phone calls from Niki, who encouraged him to use this precious time for reflection and contemplation. Niki had helped Jan view such physical intrusions as a hidden dialogue between body and psyche—a period of adjustment and absorption. If only he had begun all this thirty years ago! Two months later Jan was sailing again on his beloved Puget Sound, accompanied by plentiful Russian sailboat lovers. To return the favor, they later took him out into the fine sailing waters around Vladivostok, famous for its lineage of Olympic-class yachtsmen. Jan also found time to ski in the Cascades and also in the new resort centers built from American money in the mountains north of Vladivostok. By now he felt he was a true citizen of both East and West.

As Jan reached seventy-two, so all his life themes reached a stage of natural convergence and completion. By now he had made enough progress in his inner work to view his life more objectively. He could see he was rounding out his life. The edifice was built; all it needed now was a touch here, a touch there. Esperanza was now twelve, and Jan was permitted to take her overseas with him where she could live for six months with Natalya. Jan knew Esperanza would flourish in the special warmth of the larger family, while studying at the Vladivostok Steiner School.

Jan had his own apartment in Vladivostok but preferred to stay with Niki, where he could revivify his soul and intellect with the never-ending flow of new ideas and lively conversation. Niki's apartment was now a mecca for both Russian and American doctors, artists, musicians, writers, and even young priests. The crowded room expressed the surge of a new kind of thinking, not coldly clever and abstract, but rather an enlivening union of heart and mind—there was warmth in it. Jan, as usual, never said much—but how he listened! No mind could ever atrophy in such a place.

Soon the council would reach its final decision on Jan's urban project, now capably developed by his son Theo, working in concert with the local architects. Theo now had many Russian friends and had also begun to view his old dad with a reserved but growing measure of warmth and respect, not from personal communication, but from the obvious gratitude the Soviets had for his father's work. His brother Diaz spent most of his time in the local Immigration Department and had taken up the challenging offer to teach a law course at the college.

Jan felt the constriction mount as his anxieties about the next day's council decision fluttered uneasily among his emotions. He had devoted years of work to this five-hundred-acre project, now fully modernized and adapted to the local conditions and requirements.

Niki, aware of his old friend's edginess, suggested they walk again to their lighthouse, that red- and white-striped symbol of guidance, the place that always welcomed their moods of solitude or sharing. They sat for a while in silence, peering eastward into the hazy mask of infinity, the sun setting behind the hills at their backs. The unusual quietude of the elements was perfectly attuned to a mood of repose. Thus, they sat on the rocks, each within himself.

Niki suddenly broke the composure. "Jan, perhaps the art of patience, the self-assurance necessary to greet the future flowing into the present, is to trust its wisdom. Try to welcome it with unconditional acceptance. The future, despite its mystery, is never disconnected from your interior self, never really external but already at work somewhere in your deeper regions. The future, as potential in process of becoming reality, always casts both its shadow and its light before it. Imagine the currents of past and future combining to create the genesis of the present within the hidden crucible we call soul. Everything will go well, my friend, come what may."

Jan made no comment. Recent years had cultivated his ability to let Niki's ideas percolate through the strata of his mind, unimpeded by intellectual speculation, to seek their own destination. Speaking to the oceanic image of infinity before them, Niki recalled his own history of persecution and oppression, the rage generated by the brutal suppression of freedom of thought and expression. "I have lost so many dear friends to the Gulag, Jan, but this pain has taught me to overview my panorama of anguish as a sequence of gifts, yes, the pearls of great price formed by so much irritation in the oyster I call my soul. In other words, these sufferings are the resistances designed to awaken and evolve my affirmation of life. I can now trust its wisdom. Each of my wounds has contributed to my personal transformation—and I value them. In some strange way I have been protected—but never from the pain."

Niki emphasized the point. "My world view has no place for the word *accident*. This is a ghost powerless to stand the light of close examination. Every failure, I am convinced, every rebuff or stroke of so-called bad fortune has its meaningful position in my life's quest. Thus, I see the experiential world as nothing less than my treasure fields and my spiritual confidence is the harvest of my past travail. Now I can willingly share the pain of others."

Niki then made a specific request—something he had never done before with Jan. He asked Jan to make a full appraisal of his life's path, urging him to examine its complex patterns, marking the crucial events, disturbances, crises, and victories. "After this, Jan, try to recollect them as a whole, even as a glorious synthesis of self-creation to be observed objectively without recrimination, without emotion. See yourself moving through the world's space, expressing, building, creating yourself in it. This exercise will awaken your sense of path, a path you can never desert, a path bereft of purpose? No, not for a millisecond. In time," he added, "you will discover for yourself how all your formative experiences scavenged through your years have fashioned the whole superstructure of your existence. Once you visualize the composite time picture of your journey, you can then confidently tackle your most recalcitrant problem—your father's unique place in the scheme of things."

Jan flinched for an instant. Here it was at last. Niki was about to touch his most sensitive nerve. But Niki was well aware of Jan's still-open wound. He smiled and reached out to touch Jan's hand, as it gripped the rock beside him. "Please rest assured, my old friend, that your father, like everyone else, formed his decisions from the best consciousness he could muster at the time. He could not do otherwise. By observing your life's journey, you will eventually uncover the truth that Willem has been the major reagent in the whole alchemy of your life and all its themes. Willem helped to form the bedrock of your destiny and provided, albeit unconsciously, so many impulses to give it both direction and meaning.

"Please try to search the corridors of your time to identify the doors your 'adversaries' have opened for you. Your 'enemies' are, in truth, your benefactors, guides, pathfinders, the wise kings following your star of destiny for a while as you have followed theirs. Yes, all have served you faithfully with their gifts of love and anguish. If only you could hold fast to this truth, you will forgive, even revere them, one and all. You will even forgive your father, who has trespassed against you. In so doing, he helped to generate the drive responsible for your striving, your life's path. Above all, this recognition will enable you to forgive yourself. Thus will your weight of shame and guilt find true absorption and redemption. Thus does the mystery of time bring forth the pain and then the healing. True self-acceptance will bring acceptance of the other, and the 'I' and the 'Thou' can then meet in concord.

"Please be vigilant on this mental journey, Jan. See how your adversaries brought you to America, to Tbilisi, to this lighthouse! Each of them placed their offerings on the altar of your manhood. I know it is immensely difficult, but try to recognize and acknowledge the value of the pain they gave you, and you them. All those horrors belong to your covenant of awakening. Accept them, and release them. When you meet again, you will offer them more warmth than heat, more giving than needing, more love than hate."

Niki had said what had to be said. It was done. The gift was given—in freedom. In the silence that followed, Niki and Jan both sank themselves into the musing tranquility of twilight for a time before making their way back through the dew-laden grass.

Later, while pondering Niki's words to the rhythmic play of his flickering bedside candle, Jan felt himself filled with the warmth of Niki's nourishment. He pledged himself to work with these thoughts every morning. He was ready for tomorrow's council decision and knew he would accept the wisdom of its verdict—whatever it might be.

The following evening Jan found himself totally drained. It had been a long, strenuous day. Despite his wavering attention span, he had enjoyed himself at the council meeting. What a glorious day it had been. How these Russians loved their rituals and ceremony! The large conference room had been filled with people. After numerous introductions, the council president formally accepted the inner-housing project with its family clinics, council, and cultural facilities. The president went on to express profound gratitude for the American expertise, advanced medical technology, and training donated by the city of Tacoma. Jan was then called to the platform to receive the mayor's Medal of Honor and the Freedom of the City. Theo also received a plaque of commendation. Jan, with throat narrowed by emotion, haltingly thanked them all—in Russian. This was all he could say.

He knew his work was in good, capable, and creative Russian-American hands. He loved them, these old enemies who had once tried to obliterate him long ago in Hungary. He loved their freshness of spirit, their remarkable love for their soil. He trusted them.

Stretching his aching back and limbs, Jan walked slowly up the winding path above his apartment, where he could overlook the great port of Vladivostok. Perhaps he might see his favorite place in the distance—the friendly sentinel of Basargin Cape.

It was an exquisite fall evening, muted by the suffused orange hues of sunset. Halfway up the steep incline, Jan rested himself on a bench to peruse the harbor view below, where vessels from widespread lands, many of them with

American flags, contentedly rode at anchor. As the shadows eased their fingers among the hulls and piers, so the veil of night softened and slowed the bustle and pace of the commercial day. Somewhere down there his daughter and Natalya were enjoying their evening meal. Jan knew Esperanza was happy and growing well. Somewhere down there in the broadening shadows his son Diaz was about to teach American law at the evening college, and Theo was no doubt celebrating Jan's triumph with his Russian colleagues. A soft breeze brushed the left side of Jan's face as he closed his eyes.

Gently, the image of his father composed itself unannounced on the screen of his mind, an image free from its usual discomfort and rancor. Jan felt he could freely offer the blessings of his triumph to Willem. He knew that his own victory was his father's, too, and he could share its blessings with him. Yes, he, the son, was an extension of the father, whose own place in time and space could not offer the opportunities bestowed on the son. Jan was left with the warmth of this offering as the image dissolved. Perhaps his father would receive Jan's gift, wherever he was.

The cry of a lone gull, wheeling invisible, woke Jan. The night cloak, wrapping itself around him unawares, had covered everything except a razor-thin slash of deep crimson across the western horizon. Where was he? Was this the harbor of Rotterdam? Was it the port of Tacoma or Vladivostok? No matter. Jan felt himself slip into a warm pool of wholeness and harmony. Yet, as always, the voice of his mind rose to prompt him. *What needs to be done tomorrow? There is so much work to be done, so many arrangements to be made.* But Jan could not think of a thing. Nothing at all. Nothing whatsoever.

* * *

I am Chronos, and I have offered my story. Let us now review it.

Within each of my great thirty-year cycles, many events are inscribed. You may well inquire if their particular placement and sequence also obey my ordinance of time. Yes, indeed, my primary rhythm contains many others. Let us briefly consider two of them.

Look at your own timepath and you should detect the presence of my twelve-year rhythm, which translates your emerging self-identity into the sequential stages of your life's work. This cycle, in particular, orchestrates the phases of scientific, artistic, or philosophical growth, whatever your career might be. The working of the twelve is evident in the maturing of ideas, spans of personal relationships, even those strokes of good fortune when something "clicks" for you, when something beneficial and expansive comes to meet you at just the propitious moment. This is my rhythm of creativity. It is especially prevalent in the lives of creative people. Call it the "career cycle" and be optimistic when you reach its nodes at twelve or twenty-four, thirty-six, forty-eight, and so on. It shapes the structure of your career and lifts your life themes through a sequence of ever-maturing stages. In Jan's case, we saw his medical studies at twenty-four, his first constructive project at Moreland at thirty-six, becoming a manager at forty-eight, his retirement, design competition, soccer interest, and the Physicians' exchange Project at sixty, his grand conclusion in Vladivostok when he was seventy-two. So did the star of Jan's destiny rise to its culmination under the sway of this rhythm.

Also inscribed within my great cycles is the indispensable seven-year "cycle of individuation," so named since it coordinates the emergence of your self-identity, your psychological relationship to yourself and world. It controls the digestion of experience and its psychological effects. Thus, it orchestrates your crises, ever transmuting your experience into the essence of who you are. This is the rhythm of individuality. Examine well the change of consciousness at seven, the pubertal changes at fourteen, the emergence of egohood at twenty-one. This rhythm will continue to draw the past into the present at the ordained cyclic moments for re-examination, correction, and re-absorption. Yes, you may well call it the Cycle of Individuation, since it coordinates all phases of your growth as an individual. This is why the seven is a vital agent in the cycles of psychological crisis.

Recall the working of the seven in Jan's timelife. At fourteen, the upheaval of the German invasion; at twenty-one, his admittance to the military hospital; at twenty-eight, the struggle to complete his degree; at thirty-five, his return to Holland; at forty-two, his Vietnam dilemmas; at forty-nine, his family conflict; at fifty-six, his divorce; at sixty-three his breakdown; at seventy, his illness. All these years were nodes of tension, times when Jan's interior disturbance and change triggered his crises.

The tale is told, the life disclosed, in trust, some courage given, and light revealed.

In the name of your self-aspiring, I urge you to evaluate your life path and identify these rhythms permeating your body, soul, and spirit. Thus, will you waken your time intelligence and marvel at my wisdom embedded in it. Yes, I am the choreographer, arranging, proportioning the patterns of your dance through time.

Lest you be unsure, let me here define my use of "soul" and "spirit"—the difference thereof. By spirit, I indicate the indivisible, nuclear center of your reality. It is the *knower* in you, that which empowers your grasp for experience, that which evolves in you. It is the timelessness in your time. But while you stride through eternity, your soul circles in its rhythms. Soul is your faculty of sentience, your capacity to feel. It ensheathes your spirit kernel. Soul is the *relator* in you, which connects you to both the world without and the interior of your psyche. Through your soul you share the lives of other souls, the soul of your nation, the soul of your planet. Through your soul you breathe the life currents of the world.

Before I leave you, let me condense my instruction. An evolution devoid of destiny is meaningless, a mere spiral of incidentals remote from personal freedom. Beware, then, the nihilistic mind that would clasp you in its carrion claws of circumstance and accident. Its dark power can only devalue, disintegrate, and separate all it touches. Yes, meaninglessness in self and planet is the most dreadful threat of all. Look rather to destiny as freedom in becoming for the only justification for the impediments, trials, and miseries of existence.

According to the greater rhythms of the aeons, as social structures dissolve so shall the emergent self feel stranded in isolation, separation, and acute loneliness. But fear not. This pain is but the genesis of new forms of community, new social interworkings built on the freedom of the self, not imposed by the rule of authority.

As you sharpen your sense of destiny, so shall you unlock your compassion for the oppressed and the wretched, squirming in their Sisyphean torment. Thus will the down-trodden draw ever more compassion from the awakening capacities of human ascendance. Remember well, only an individual can intuit the individuality of others. As the self uncovers meaning in destiny, so shall it acknowledge its meaning for others. Thus, through the gyrations of time, love will yet manifest its highest, its truest creations.

Be assured, the universe has unlimited compassion for your perils and travail. Know that suffering is naught but your self-sought investment in the immensity of your potential to live, to evolve. Without destiny, both life and its pain are utterly worthless. Take comfort from the words of C. S. Lewis: "Pain is God's megaphone to rouse a deaf world." I say to you, your awakening sense of destination will draw self, community, and planet closer to concord and mutuality. Consider, too, the thought of Mother Maria: "Time is a ship which carries thee, it is not thy home." And this is not your maiden voyage!

Yes, so it is. Destiny is your heroic search for the good and true whereby you shall fill eternity and make it personal. Through this you shall transform its wisdom into love. Dwell on this mystery. I send you the blessings of your time.

> Your servant,
> Chronos

INDIVIDUAL PSYCHOLOGICAL CRISES
7 YEAR CYCLE – [0-42]

0	7	14	21	28	35	42
	Montessori	Gymnasium Exam WWII	Delft War Neurosis Interrogations	M.D. Leyden Exam	Holland Revisited	Board Exam
Sport Competition		Home Beach/ Dunes	Marriage Rowing Crew Laga Stroke		Ski Crystal Mountain	Vietnam War
			Sailboat			Cal 34 Sailboat Dutch Flute

7 YEAR CYCLE – [49-92]

49	56	63	70	77	84	92
Recert Exam	Recert Exam	Burn out Depression Stress Syndrome	Heart Condition	Meditation		
Welfare Fraud	Divorce					
Bart Finance		Ethics Biofeedback				
Sail Ski Racing	Tennis	Goodwill Physicians Exchange				
	Ski Sun Valley Soccer Stars	Design Competition				

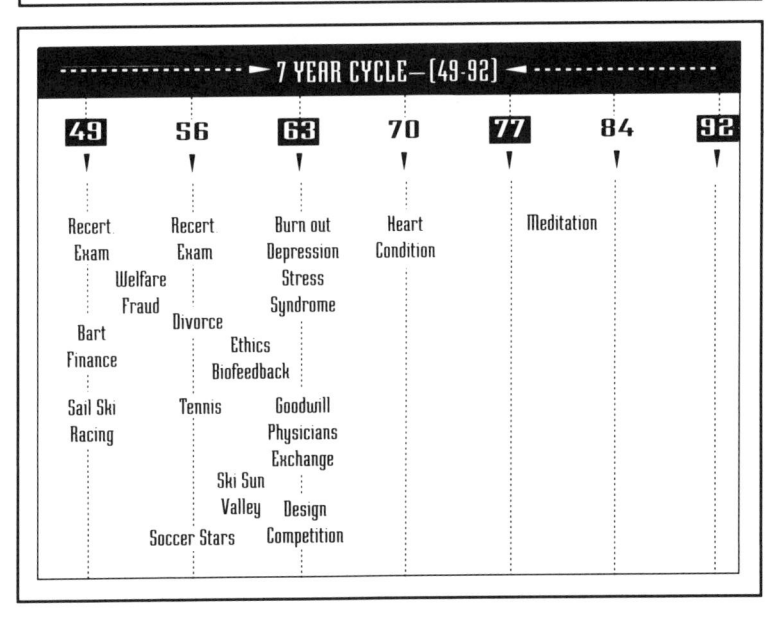

CAREER
12 YEAR CYCLE

0	12	24	36	48	60	72	84
	Gymnasium Haarlem	Leyoen Medicine	Allenmore Medical Center	Recertification Seattle	Personal Injuries Legal	Russia Medical Building	
Montessori Haarlem	Delft Naval Architecture	TGH Intern Tacoma	Board Certification New York	Recertification Portland	Seattle Design Comp		
	Gymnasium Haarlem		House	Puget Tower Apartments		Sheffield Apt	Medal of Honor and Freedom to the City of Vladvosk
Evert T-Ford			Crystal Mt Ski Cabin	Allenmore Center Management	N Light House Condo		
				Allenmore Ridge Condo Lake Chelan Hi Tide Ocean			

LIFE SPAN
30 YEAR CYCLE

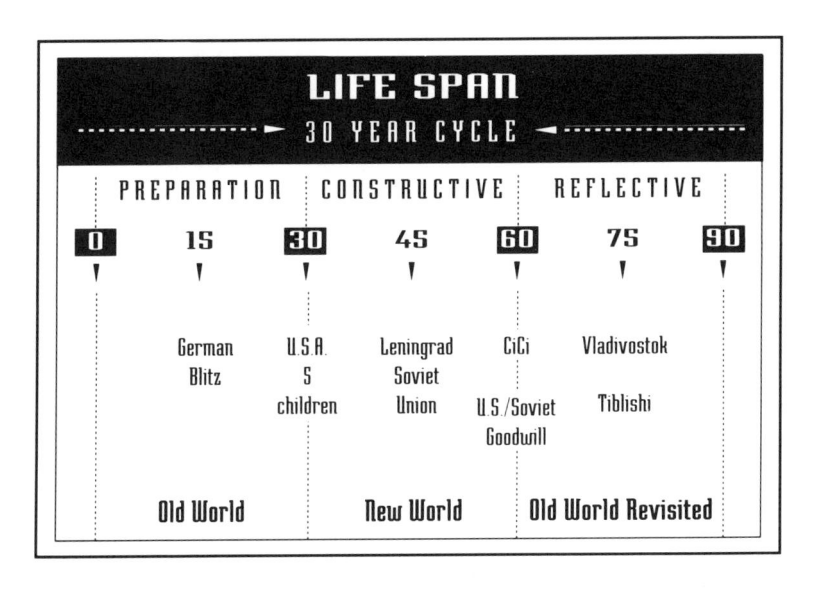

PREPARATION	CONSTRUCTIVE	REFLECTIVE

0   15   **30**   45   **60**   75   **90**

German Blitz	U.S.A. 5 children	Leningrad Soviet Union	CiCi U.S./Soviet Goodwill	Vladivostok Tiblishi

Old World   **New World**   **Old World Revisited**

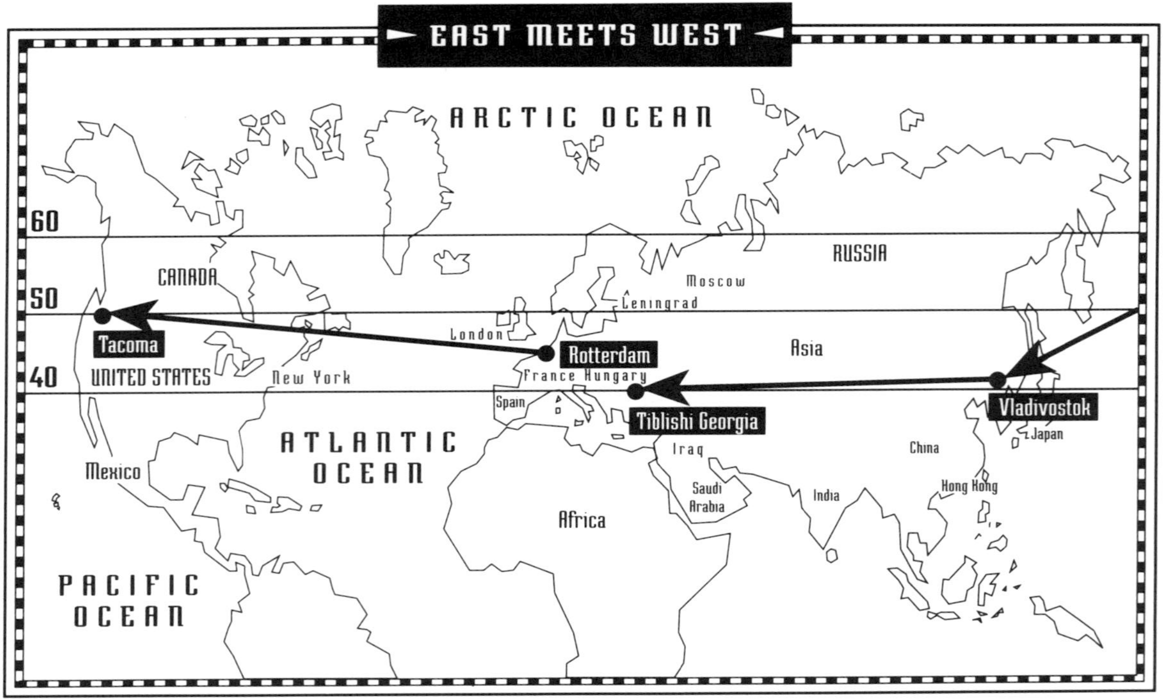
EAST MEETS WEST
ARCTIC OCEAN
60
50
40
CANADA
UNITED STATES
Tacoma
New York
Mexico
ATLANTIC OCEAN
PACIFIC OCEAN
London
Rotterdam
France
Hungary
Spain
Leningrad
Moscow
RUSSIA
Asia
Tiblishi Georgia
Iraq
Saudi Arabia
Africa
India
China
Hong Kong
Vladivostok
Japan

THE CHRONOS DIRECTIVE

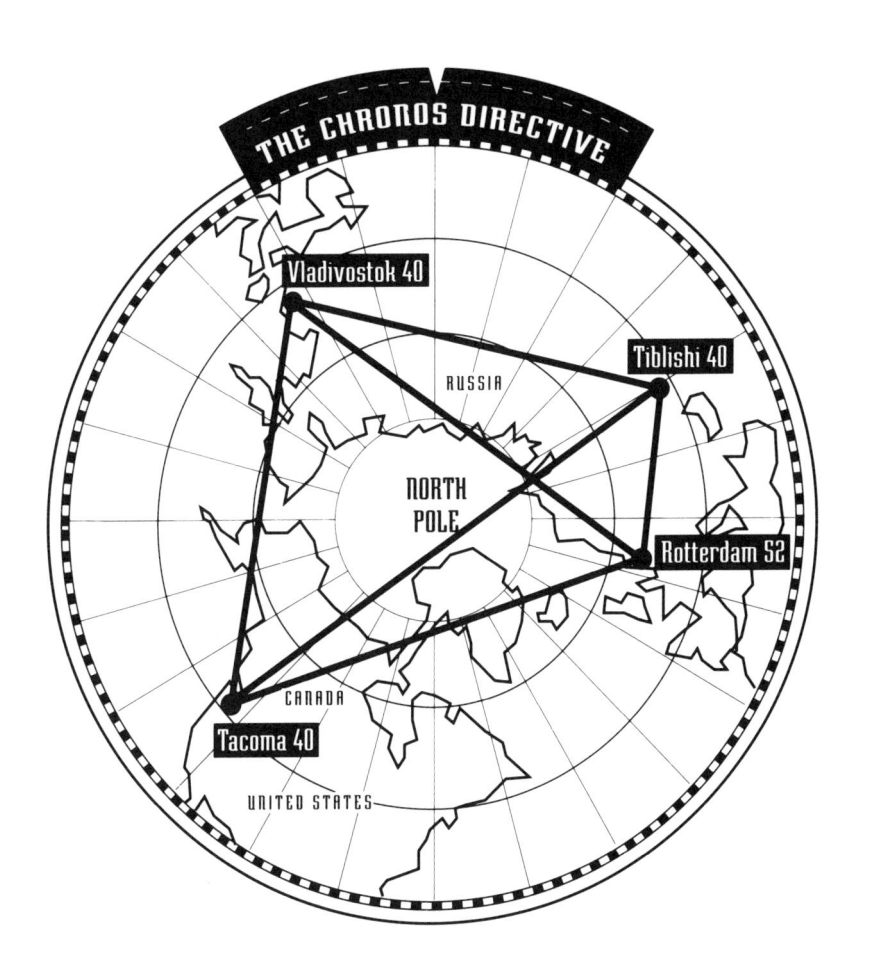

Vladivostok 40

Tiblishi 40

RUSSIA

Rotterdam 52

NORTH POLE

CANADA

Tacoma 40

UNITED STATES